TM and the Missing Coed

Action And Adventure As The Search For A Missing Coed Leads To Murder And Financial And International Intrigue

CORDELL OVERGAARD

Other Novel Published by Cordell Overgaard

TM and the Little White Dog

ISBN: 0615845142
ISBN-13: 9780615845142
Library of Congress Control Number: 2013912426
CreateSpace Independent Publishing Platform
North Charleston, South Carolina

This is a work of fiction. Names, characters, places, and incidents either are the product of the author's imagination or are used fictitiously, and any resemblance to actual persons living or dead is entirely coincidental.

1

As Carol Ryan walked along Butler Avenue in Flagstaff, Arizona, near the university campus, she was pleased with her appearance, even though her jacket and pants concealed her numerous tattoos. Her short, bright purple hair was visible from a distance, and someone near her would have been able to see the snake tooth piercings on her lower lip. Carol was very proud of her piercings. They were difficult to administer and painful to endure, but none of her friends, with all their facial artistry, had anything as elegant.

Of course there were drawbacks to her appearance. More than one prospective employer had rejected her—not with a word but with a look of disdain. But thanks to a friend, she had found a job with a fast food restaurant. She wore a black wig and temporarily defanged the snake.

Carol had finished two years of classes at the university and then dropped out. That was eight months ago. She had stopped communicating with her parents, who seemed not to care. They had their own problems—they fought most of the time—and were relieved to stop the flow of checks to the university, her landlord, and Carol herself. No longer did they worry about the guilt trip society placed on middle-income parents who denied their children a college education.

Admittedly Carol's life was not as comfortable as before. Her dorm room had been pleasant and her roommate acceptable. She'd had hot meals at breakfast, lunch, and dinner and a vending machine for snacks. Now she lived in a basement room with two other dropouts and mostly ate fast food that had caused her weight to balloon to 140 pounds on her five-foot-three-inch frame. But she was happier than she had ever been. She had more in common with her new roommates and felt much less pressure than before. They were always able to get an ample supply of marijuana, and sometimes they made extra money by selling it to others even though the markup was not very great. They lived for today and sometimes tomorrow. The future would take care of itself.

Carol loved Flagstaff. The San Francisco peaks and the ponderosa pines overcame the run-down, unattractive old motels on Route 66. And the sunsets frequently were a photographer's dream. She also liked the people in Flagstaff. They were more down-to-earth and less materialistic than the people in the town where her parents lived. She had even grown used to the monsoons in late July and August, when the rainstorms could be quite severe.

It was getting dark as Carol turned the corner and headed south on South Agassiz Street. The street was deserted, and the only light came from rooms in nearby buildings. When Carol reached Dupont Street and headed west, a car stopped and blocked her path. She recognized the car and the driver. The driver lowered his window and said a few words to Carol. Without hesitation, she walked around the front of the car and slid into the passenger seat. She closed the door, and the car drove off.

2

Bob and Mary Carson looked forward all week to their weekend trail ride in the Coconino National Forest. It was beginning to get hot in the valley, and the cooler weather in the Flagstaff area would be a relief. They were able to leave work early on a Friday, which meant they would have two full days of trail riding. Driving his Ford F-150 crew cab, Bob pulled their two-horse stock trailer off US 89 onto Elden Spring Road to the Little Elden Spring Horse Camp.

Bob stopped at the entrance, paid the weekend fee, and drove to an empty space near the edge of the camp. He pulled open the rear door and backed out his pride and joy, an eight-year-old bay quarter horse gelding named Lucky. He tied Lucky to a tie-out line and went back to get Mary's horse, a fifteen-year-old chestnut quarter horse named Earl. He tied Earl to the tie-out line with enough slack so he could reach hay on the ground but not close enough to reach Lucky, who was busy eating his own flake of hay. Bob filled two buckets with water and placed one of them within reach of each horse.

Bob unhooked the trailer, and they drove into Flagstaff and had dinner at a restaurant in the Flagstaff Mall. When they returned to the horse camp, they set up a tent next to the trailer and cuddled up in a double sleeping bag for the night.

The next morning Mary fed and watered the horses, and they used a portable propane stove to cook scrambled eggs and bacon.

"What's the plan for today, trail boss?" Mary asked.

"There's a trail on the side of Mount Elden that leads to Schultz Tank, which is near a pond farther up the mountain," Bob replied. "When we get there we can decide whether to keep going to the other side of the mountain or head in a different direction. I'll have my GPS so we won't get lost and can find our way back."

"Will our cell phones work?"

"Mine works now, but who knows whether it will work as we climb the mountain. Why do you ask? Are you planning to go off on your own?"

"Of course not, silly," Mary said. "But I always feel more comfortable if I can call someone in an emergency. Are we likely to come across any rattlesnakes?"

"I doubt it, but we could spot a mountain lion."

"Are you serious, Bob?" Mary cried.

"Not really. But we might see an elk. There are lots of them in these woods."

After tending to the horses' hooves and brushing their bodies, tails, and manes, Bob and Mary saddled them up and were on their way. With Lucky in the lead, they walked through the trees and across Elden Spring Road until they came to Little Elden Spring Trail. They headed in a westerly direction up the side of the mountain.

"This is magnificent," Mary exclaimed. "The pines are so beautiful, and look at those gorgeous trees with white bark."

"They're aspen trees," Bob replied. "They have strong root systems that support new trees even after a fire. The leaves of the aspen tree turn yellowish-gold in the fall and are stunning."

"Show-off! How do you know all this?"

"I'm just smart," Bob said, laughing. "That's why you married me."

"I thought there was a reason," Mary said.

After several minutes, they came to a place where the trail narrowed and there was a steep drop-off to their right.

"Bob, I don't like this one bit," Mary shouted. "What if someone comes in the opposite direction on a horse?"

"Let's hope they don't," Bob exclaimed. "It should get better soon."

After a few minutes, the trail widened and the horses proceeded at a walk until they reached the pond, where there were other people on horseback. Bob and Mary got off the horses and sat on a grassy hill to enjoy the scenery. They noticed that even though it was the beginning of May, there was still snow at the top of the peaks.

"Where do we go now?" Mary asked.

"We can keep going between the mountaintops on the Schultz Creek Trail or go back the way we came," Bob replied.

"There's no way I'll go back next to the cliff. But if we keep going, it'll take us a long time to get back. Aren't there any other trails near the camp?"

"I'm sure there are. We can take a different way back. Elden Spring Road is just over that little hill. We can take the road back, but we'll have to be careful about cars. We might be able to ride in the forest next to the road."

"Let's do that. I'd rather watch out for cars than risk falling off a cliff. And there can't be that much traffic on the dirt road."

They led the horses to the edge of the pond, hoping they would take a drink. But the horses showed no interest in drinking. After a few minutes, they climbed back onto the saddles and headed for the road.

After they rode for a short distance, Bob led Lucky over a small ridge on the side of the road and into the trees with Mary following on Earl. Although there was no trail, the trees were far enough apart so they could ride between them.

They had ridden only a short distance when Mary suddenly screamed.

"What's the matter?" Bob shouted.

"I saw something, Bob. Come back here!" Mary shouted.

Bob wheeled Lucky around and soon was next to Mary.

"What did you see?" he asked.

"Look over there. Isn't that a hand?"

3

Jeffery T. Morgan's office in Wilmette, Illinois, was not as sumptuous as would be expected of a highly successful hedge fund manager. Morgan was in his late fifties and very distinguished looking, with his thick black hair that had streaks of gray along the sides. After graduating from Harvard Business School, he had worked for a large New York investment banking firm for a few years and then went to work for a new hedge fund that became very successful. He became a principal and enjoyed earnings in the seven to eight figures.

Two things had led to his decision to locate his office in the suburbs of Chicago: He went through a painful divorce in New York that caused him to rethink his priorities. He was also born and raised in the Chicago area and had become disenchanted with the New York lifestyle.

Because of his contacts, he was able to start his own hedge fund and continued to generate substantial income. Morgan remarried, and he and his second wife lived in a spacious home in the Chicago suburb of Kenilworth, which was known for its wealthy residents.

Morgan had a worried look on his face when his secretary escorted in Daniel Webster, Morgan's lawyer. Webster was in his early sixties but looked a lot younger. He wore a custom-tailored dark blue suit without a rear vent, a heavily starched white shirt, and a striped Ferragamo tie with a matching pocket handkerchief. His thick hair was naturally dark brown, but his eyesight had been aided by LASIK surgery.

"So what have you found out about Natalie?" Morgan asked anxiously. "Her mother is worried to death."

"My trip to Flagstaff was unsuccessful. No one at the university knew what happened to her, and none of her classmates I talked to did either. Her room looked like it still had most of her things. She seems to have disappeared without a trace."

"So we're nowhere? You have nothing to report?" Morgan said in a loud, indignant voice.

"Well, there's one possibility, but not a very good one."

"What is it?" Morgan exclaimed.

"They found a body in the forest about five miles out of town."

"Was it Natalie?"

"No, it wasn't."

"So what does it have to do with Natalie?"

"I hate to say this, but there's always the possibility a serial killer is in the area and there are more bodies to be found."

"That seems pretty farfetched. Didn't they search the area?"

"They searched the immediate area, but I don't think they were very thorough. Crimes in national forests are under the jurisdiction of the US Forest Service's Law Enforcement and Investigations unit, known as LE&I. It's spread very thin and has very limited manpower, particularly because of recent budget cuts."

"Didn't they call in the local police?"

"No. We asked them to, but they said the local authorities were stretched thin also. They said it wasn't at all unusual to find bodies in the national forest, and if they had to do an intensive search in every case, they wouldn't have time to do anything else."

"So what do you suggest?"

"It certainly seems unlikely that Natalie was a victim of a serial killer, but we can't rule that out. It comes down to how far we want to go with our search for Natalie. In spite of our best efforts, we haven't been able to locate her. I suggest we get a private firm to come in and do a search."

"What kind of firm? Private investigators or former FBI agents?"

"We need a firm that's used to hunting for bodies and has dogs trained to hunt for them."

"How do we find such a firm?"

"We've located a firm in Colorado that's been highly recommended."

"Tell me about it."

"It's called Security Services and is headed by a man named TM."

"How do you spell that?"

"A T and an M."

"Those are initials, not a name."

"No, that's his name—TM. Some people call him The Man."

"That's ridiculous, Dan. What else do you know about him?"

"He's educated. He has a degree in psychology from the University of Colorado. After graduation, he joined the army, went to officers' candidate school, and was commissioned a lieutenant. He went through Ranger training and was sent to Afghanistan just after nine/eleven. He was seriously injured in a firefight and was hospitalized in the States for several weeks. I'm told he recovered nicely and that a slight limp is the only sign of his injury."

"And he has dogs trained to find bodies?" Morgan asked.

"Yes, and as I said, he's been highly recommended."

"By whom?"

"Law enforcement people I know and respect."

"Have you talked to him?"

"No. I wanted to get your OK first."

"Go ahead and talk to him, Dan, and if he's any good, hire him. But one thing."

"What's that?"

"I hope he fails."

TM's business was located on a fifteen-acre parcel in the foothills of the Rocky Mountains a few miles from Boulder, Colorado. The parcel had two buildings; the one containing thirty-five hundred square feet was TM's home. The other was a twenty-five thousand–square-foot building that contained, in addition to a reception area and five offices, a large area similar to a gymnasium and at one end, a series of small compartments facing a corridor on one side and fenced walkouts on the other. The property also had a four-stall barn with a tack room, a feed room, and a wash rack. The stalls had twenty-foot walkouts, and the doors to the stalls were open at the top so the horses could put their heads out. A lean-to for storing hay and shavings was located a few feet from the barn. The rear area was fenced in, but a gate led to open fields that had miles of trails for riding.

TM operated two businesses from the facility. One business hired, trained, and placed security personnel to safeguard high-profile business executives, sports figures, entertainers, and others. TM did not allow his security personnel to carry firearms without specific authorization from him. Instead, the emphasis was on training security people to use personal defense techniques, such as karate, to physically deal with people who posed a risk to the person being protected.

The other business performed canine training. Dogs were trained to detect explosive material, drugs, and cadavers. The market for the dogs was relatively small, but because there were very few people or firms that could supply specially trained dogs, it was not at all unusual for a well-trained dog to be sold for several thousand dollars. Dogs trained to find cadavers were not sold but hired out for substantial fees or used on a volunteer basis for major disasters.

Morgan had arranged for Webster to fly in a Citation I private jet from Chicago Executive Airport northwest of Chicago to the Boulder airport, where he was met by a limousine service. Webster had called for an appointment and arrived a few minutes early.

TM, who was in his early forties and was slightly over six feet tall, was wearing jeans and a black jacket over an open -collar light blue shirt. He had dark brown hair and brown eyes and appeared to be in as good a shape as when he was a ranger.

"You didn't tell me much during our phone conversation about what you want," TM said.

"I represent a very wealthy man whose daughter, Natalie, has disappeared. She was a graduate student at the university in Flagstaff, and no one knows where she is now.

After she disappeared, a body was found in the national forest not far from the university. The body was not that of my client's daughter, but it raised the possibility that she may have been another victim of a serial killer."

"What gives you that idea? Was the body that of a student at the university?"

"The authorities haven't been able to identify the body, but it was a female about the same age as Natalie."

"How do you know it wasn't Natalie?"

"They were able to determine it was an Asian woman, which ruled out Natalie. Look, we don't know where to turn, but we at least want to rule out the possibility that Natalie was killed by the same person who killed the woman found in the forest."

"So what do you want us to do?"

"We want you to search the area to make sure Natalie's body isn't lying there somewhere."

"How big an area? The forest is huge. We could spend a few people's lifetimes out there."

"The body was found near a road, and we would only expect you to search on either side of the road for a few hundred feet."

"Why haven't the local authorities done that?"

"The Forest Service investigators said they didn't have the resources to conduct a speculative search for bodies."

"You mean LE&I?"

"Yes."

"We can't go into the forest and conduct a search without LE&I's approval. Do you have it?"

"No. I didn't think it was necessary. But before we go further, I need to know how much you'd charge for a search."

"I would send two of my men with two dogs for as long as it takes. The charge would be fifteen hundred dollars a day plus expenses."

"Would you be one of the men?"

"No," TM said.

"That won't work. I got my client to agree to do this because of you. You would have to be involved."

"I think you'd be better off with the two men I'd send, but if I go, the charge is two thousand a day plus expenses."

"How many days would it take?"

"That depends on so many different things that I can't give you a definite number."

"What different things?"

"The temperature, the type of terrain we'd be dealing with, and the wind direction, to name a few. And the dogs aren't robots. They have days when they need rest."

"If there's a body in the area you'll be searching, what are the odds you'll find it?"

"The best I can say is better than fifty-fifty, but I hesitate even to say that. There are so many things to be considered. How long has the body been there? Have any predators taken it away? Has the killer taken any steps to prevent detection? Are the dogs doing their best? Are we working the dogs correctly? All I can say is that we have a good track record, and we would do our very best."

"How soon could you go there?"

"We'd need three days. But you would first have to get permission from LE&I for us to do the search. And they would need to have personnel available to secure a crime scene if we find a body."

"Why?"

"We're not a law enforcement agency, and our continued involvement at the scene where a body is found could prejudice the chances of successfully prosecuting a killer."

"I'll talk to my client and get back to you."

"That's fine. But we'll need a lot more information if your client decides to go forward. For starters, we'll want recent photos of

Natalie and a DNA sample. Does she have any tattoos, birthmarks, or other distinguishing bodily characteristics?"

"That's premature. Hopefully you won't find a body and that information will be irrelevant."

"No one would feel better than me if we conduct a good search and don't find anything," TM said.

The waiting limousine took Webster to the Boulder airport, where he boarded the Citation I for the return trip to the Chicago Executive Airport. When he was back in his office, he called Roger Craig, the LE&I agent in Flagstaff he had previously talked to. He did not like what he heard.

"We can't let people come in and root around the forest, particularly when they aren't law enforcement people," Craig forcefully said.

"They wouldn't be 'rooting around.' They wouldn't disturb the ground unless they found something," Webster said.

"But their work could interfere with other people's enjoyment of the forest."

"That's nonsense," Webster shouted into the phone. "Who's your superior?"

"The special agent in charge of region three, and don't shout at me, Mr. Webster," Craig angrily said.

Craig was still seething about Webster's comments when the phone rang again.

"Hello?"

"Roger Craig?"

"Yes. Who's calling?"

"My name is TM, and I'm the person who'd be leading the search of the area in the Coconino National Forest where a body was found. I'm sorry about the somewhat hostile phone conversation you had a few minutes ago. Mr. Webster was out of line. My company has worked successfully with several law enforcement agencies, and I'm sure we can work well with you. In fact, it can be very much to your benefit for us to be involved."

"Why is that?"

"The search would be very unobtrusive, and if nothing turns up, very few people would even know or care that we were there. But if we find something bad, you'd be the winner."

"I don't understand."

"As you know, we're not a law enforcement agency. The first thing we would do if we found signs of a body is to contact you. You would be the one to hold a press conference and announce the news. You would get credit for bringing in outside experts to conduct the search."

"Are you sure the search would be unobtrusive?"

"Definitely. The last thing we'd want is to have a crowd watching what we do. It makes it much more difficult to work the dogs. I see no downside for you and potentially a big upside. When can we get started?"

"Well," Craig said hesitantly, "when would you expect to be here?"

"Next Monday. We'll come to your office and you can fill us in on the details about the recovery of the previous body."

"OK, but I didn't catch your name, only your initials."

"I'll give you my card when we get there."

4

TM and his canine manager, Jim Anderson, took turns driving the Ford F-350 crew cab short-bed diesel truck from Boulder to Flagstaff. They were pulling a two-horse, slant-load aluminum trailer that contained Rain Dancer, a seven-year-old gray Paso Fino gelding, and Sevillana, a gray eleven-year-old Paso Fino mare. On the truck's back seat were the two dogs TM and Anderson would use for their search. Nick was a four-year-old black-and-tan German shepherd male, and Jackie was a brown female Humane Society mixed-breed dog. Anderson had trained both of them to find cadavers. Jackie, who was one of TM's personal dogs and slept at the foot of his bed, was somewhat small for a cadaver dog but had an extended nose considered desirable for a scenting dog. TM thought Jackie was half border collie since she was the same size as a border collie and just as smart.

They exited Interstate 40 at the Country Club Drive exit and soon were on Highway 89 headed north. Anderson had made arrangements for them to board the horses at a stable a few miles north on Highway 89 from Elden Spring Road. The stable also had two pens for the dogs. After they fed and watered the dogs and horses, they drove to a small hotel on Country Club Drive near the Interstate 40 interchange.

The next morning TM and Anderson met with Agent Craig at the ranger station just off Highway 89 north of the Flagstaff Mall.

"I've never worked with tracking dogs before," Craig said. "How are they able to find bodies that have been buried?"

"The key is the dog's olfactory system," Anderson said. "Without getting too technical, the olfactory system is what enables both humans and dogs to detect scent. A dog's system is much larger than a human's and has many more olfactory sensory cells. A man may have five million olfactory cells while a German shepherd may have two hundred and twenty million. Among other things, this enables a dog to discriminate among various smells and detect a particular odor."

"But how can there be an odor when a body is buried?" Craig asked.

"As bodies decompose, bacteria molecules are released, which percolate up through the soil and create a scent pool. Wind and heat can then create a scent cone that decreases in concentration as it moves away from the scent pool. Also, any blood or body secretion at the surface remains detectable by a well-trained dog for months if not longer. Dogs are even used to locate people who have drowned."

"How many dogs did you bring?" Craig asked.

"Two," TM said. "We also brought two horses. We intend to use them to get a good look at the area before we start the search. Can you take us to the area where the body was found?"

"Of course."

"We'll bring the dogs in the morning."

The place where the body was found was less than thirty feet from the road. But it was in an area not visible from the road because it was lower than the surroundings and was obscured by bushes.

"What do you know about the body?" TM asked.

"It was a woman, probably in her twenties. She was about five and a half feet tall and weighed about one hundred and twenty pounds. She had several tattoos and a ring in her nose. She also had black hair but with bright yellow streaks."

"I was told she was Asian."

"Yes. Partially Asian."

"What did the autopsy show about the cause of death?"

"Strangulation," Craig replied.

"Was she raped?" TM asked.

"No. Which actually is unfortunate because we couldn't recover DNA."

6

It was 3:20 a.m. when Morgan and his wife, Jane, were awakened by the soft but persistent ringing of the phone. Morgan turned on the light on the nightstand and then picked up the phone.

"Hello?" he said softly.

"We have your daughter," a muffled voice said. "We want one million dollars in gold or you will never see your daughter again. We'll call you again with delivery instructions. *Do not call the police!* Here's your daughter. "

"Daddy! Daddy! I'm scared!" Natalie screamed, and the line went dead.

"That was Natalie," Jane shouted. "What's happened?"

"She's been kidnapped," a stunned Morgan said slowly.

"Oh my God, Jeff," Jane cried. "What can we do?"

"I don't know," Morgan said.

"What do they want?" Jane demanded.

"A million dollars in gold."

"Let's give it to them," Jane said. "Anything to get my baby back safely."

"It's not that easy, Jane," Morgan exclaimed.

"But you're a successful hedge fund manager," Jane cried. "You have access to all kinds of money, and we have substantial personal funds. We can afford a million dollars."

"We don't have a million in cash lying around, let alone a million dollars in gold. And how do we know the kidnapper will let Natalie go even if he gets the gold? The caller warned me not to call the police, but we probably should call the FBI."

"No!" Jane shouted. "We can't take the chance the caller will find out and kill Natalie."

"The FBI is experienced in dealing with kidnappers and would keep things quiet while they look for the kidnapper."

"No," Jane said firmly. "We can't take the slightest chance the kidnapper will find out."

"We can't do anything then until the kidnapper calls back with instructions. But I would at least like to talk to Webster and tell him what's happened."

"Can you trust him not to say anything?"

"Absolutely!" Morgan exclaimed.

"You have to promise me, Jeff, that you won't call the police or the FBI. Look me in the eyes and promise me," Jane tearfully said.

"I promise," Morgan said quietly.

"You need to call the FBI, Jeff," Webster said firmly as he sat in Morgan's home office at six in the morning.

"I can't, Dan," Morgan said. "I promised Jane I wouldn't call the police."

"That's insane. The FBI has years of experience in dealing with kidnappers and has huge resources it can bring to bear. It has a surveillance plane that can hover silently over an area and is virtually undetectable. It has special listening devices and can pinpoint where someone is when they make a cell phone call."

"But if they slip up at all, the kidnapper could kill Natalie."

"Sorry to say, Jeff, but that could happen anyway. The FBI is very careful and not likely to make a mistake. Besides, they can be very useful in handling the delivery of the ransom. The logistics of getting the ransom paid can be complicated," Webster said. "Particularly since the kidnapper is asking for gold."

"The question of whether we will contact the FBI is settled and not up for discussion. I know it will be complicated to get the ransom paid. That's why I called you. I need your help. Can I count on you?"

"Yes, as long as what I'm asked to do is legal and doesn't endanger my life. How do you get a million dollars' worth of gold?" Webster asked. "And how do you deliver that much gold to anyone?"

"Getting that much gold isn't easy, but it can be accomplished. Finding a way to deliver it to the kidnapper is a whole other matter."

7

TM and Anderson met Agent Craig at the search site just after daybreak. They kept the dogs in the truck while they evaluated the conditions.

"The wind isn't very strong," Anderson said, "but it seems to be coming from the southwest."

"How is the wind important?" Craig asked.

"We want the dogs to work perpendicular to the wind so they can pick up a scent cone," Anderson replied. "A scent cone is pushed by the wind, so if we work parallel to the cone, we could miss it."

TM took a handful of orange wire-mounted flags from the truck and began marking out search corridors. He started by placing a flag at the starting point and then, using a mirror-sighted compass set for the heading he wanted, walked fifty feet, where he placed a second flag. He continued another fifty feet and placed another flag. TM then walked twelve feet at a ninety-degree angle and placed a flag. He turned and walked in the opposite direction of his original heading, placing a flag after the first fifty feet and again at one hundred feet until he had created a rectangular corridor. He repeated the process until he had established four corridors.

"Why are you starting the search on the other side of the road from where the body was found?" Craig asked.

"Because this side slopes downhill, and it's easier for a person to carry a body downhill than uphill," TM said. "The place where the body was found was unusual in that it was flat and formed somewhat of a valley. It was the only flat place we could find on that side of the road."

Anderson brought Nick, the German shepherd, out of the truck and took him to the edge of the first corridor. He sat and looked at him until he softly said, "Find." Nick wagged his tail vigorously and walked slowly forward in the corridor as Anderson guided him between the flags. Anderson closely watched Nick's body language for any sign he had found something. At one point he stopped, sniffed, and then urinated. Knowing Nick as well as he did, Anderson knew Nick had found an animal odor and was marking the spot.

When they reached the end of the corridor, they moved over to the second corridor and headed back to the baseline. By the time they reached the baseline, about twenty minutes had passed since they started the search. Anderson called Nick over to the truck and let him drink from a water bowl he had placed there earlier.

"How do you decide when to rest the dog?" Craig asked.

"We follow the twenty-ten rule," TM said. "We work for twenty minutes and rest the dog for ten. If you work a dog too long at one time, he can lose his edge and be less effective."

TM's cell phone rang, and when he answered it, he heard Webster say, "My client has decided not to proceed with the search, so you can stop everything."

"So you found Natalie?" TM asked.

"My client has decided to end the search. Send me your invoice," Webster said and hung up.

"Very strange," TM said to Anderson.

"What happened?" Anderson said.

"The call was from the lawyer who hired us telling me his client decided to end the search and that I should send a bill. When I asked him whether the client's daughter had been found, he didn't respond and hung up."

"Well, I guess we load up and leave," Anderson said. "Should I tell Craig?"

"Not yet," TM replied. "Let's finish the last two corridors we marked."

Anderson brought Nick to the baseline before the third corridor and again said, "Find." They had proceeded about forty feet when Nick began to pant. He circled a small area, stopped, and wagged his tail rapidly as he looked into Anderson's eyes.

"Here," Anderson said as he called Nick to him. He then gave him a small treat from a treat bag attached to his belt.

TM, who had been watching closely, turned and yelled to the agent, who was standing several yards away. When Craig ran to him, TM said, "We may have found something. The dog reacted to a place near where Jim is standing. To be safe, we should treat it as a crime scene. Take one of our flags and put it at the edge of the place where Jim is pointing. We'll pull back, and you and your people can find out what's there."

Only a foot or so below the surface, Craig and a sheriff's deputy found the partially decomposed body of what appeared to be a young woman.

When Webster's cell phone rang, he saw the call was from TM and decided not to answer. There was nothing he could say to TM under the circumstances. He certainly didn't want to answer the question about whether Natalie had been found. Within minutes, his cell phone signaled there was a text message. He looked down and said aloud, "Oh my God." The message read, *Found another body.*

"I thought we agreed to stop the search?" an irritated Morgan said to Webster.

"We did," Webster said. "I told TM to stop, but apparently he kept searching."

"Was it Natalie's body?"

"I don't know, Jeff. All I got was a text message saying another body had been found."

"Hold on. My other phone is ringing. Hello?" Morgan said apprehensively.

"You called the police didn't you?" a muffled voice said.

"No, no," Morgan cried into the phone.

"Don't even think about doing so, or you'll never see your daughter again. Here are your instructions. You are to buy a bearer certificate for one million dollars of gold. I will call you back in two days and tell you where to deliver the certificate."

"How do I know my daughter is still alive?" Morgan asked.

"Hold on."

"Daddy! Daddy! I'm scared!" Natalie screamed.

"Now do what you're told," the muffled voice said, and the line went dead.

"Dan, Dan, are you still there?" Morgan shouted into the phone.

"Yes, I'm here. What's wrong?"

"That was the kidnapper. He wants me to buy a bearer certificate for one million dollars of gold. He said he'd call back and tell me where to deliver it."

"I've never heard of a bearer certificate for gold," Webster said.

"Actually, at one time, the US Treasury issued bearer gold certificates, but when we went off the gold standard in the early thirties, they were supposed to be surrendered. It was illegal to hold them until 1964. But there aren't many out there now. The only place I know of where you can get gold bearer certificates is Dubai, but you have to be very careful about who you deal with. My firm has good contacts there, so I should be able to get something that's legitimate."

"But how does it work?" Webster asked. "The price of gold fluctuates constantly."

"I would purchase a certificate representing the number of grams worth a million dollars on the date of purchase. The value of the certificate can go up or down as time goes on."

"The kidnapper must be pretty sophisticated to come up with a demand for bearer gold certificates," Webster said. "He also must have good contacts so he can cash them in. This is where the FBI could be very helpful."

"Stop," Morgan said firmly. "Don't bring that up again."

"You look like something else is bothering you," Webster said.

"When I asked the kidnapper whether Natalie was still alive, he put her on the phone." "So?"

"What she said and the way she said it were exactly the same as during the first call."

"Do you think it was a recording?"

"That's what worries me. I think you better find out whether the new body is Natalie."

8

TM and Anderson were loading the horses onto the horse trailer when TM's cell phone rang.

"Hello?"

"Where are you?" Craig asked in a frantic voice.

"We're at the stable where we kept the horses. We're loading the horses and dogs and will be on our way shortly back to Boulder," TM said.

"What? You can't leave now. You have to continue the search," Craig screamed.

"The people who hired us told us to stop," TM said. "So no one's paying our way. We don't work for free."

"But this is an emergency. We have to continue the search. There may be more bodies."

"If this were an emergency where someone was in imminent danger we certainly would continue," TM said. "But that's not the case. LE&I certainly has time to use its own resources or hire someone else to continue the search."

"It makes the most sense for you to continue. Give me time to contact my superiors and get authority to hire you."

"OK," TM said and ended the call.

TM's phone rang again. "Hello?"

"This is Dan Webster. Are you still in Flagstaff?"

"We're getting ready to leave."

"Don't go. I'm about to board a private jet to fly to Flagstaff to meet you."

"Are we hired again and on the clock?" TM asked.

"Absolutely," Webster replied.

The phone rang again, and this time it was Craig. "We'll pay your regular rates. When can you resume the search?"

"Tomorrow," TM said.

TM turned to Anderson and said, "Suddenly we're very popular. You better call the hotel and see if we still have our rooms."

When TM and Anderson drove to Elden Spring Road the next morning, they were pleased to see the Forest Service had closed off a large area where the bodies had been found. Security was so tight they had trouble driving into the search area. TM persuaded the deputy sheriff to call Craig, and they were quickly waved through. TM parked the truck behind Craig's Forest Service vehicle.

"Anderson is going to continue searching the remainder of the corridors we marked and additional adjacent corridors," TM told Craig. "I'm going to take the other dog and do a hasty search in a different area."

"Why does it have to be a hasty search?" Craig asked.

"When we were on horseback, I noticed some dirt roads intersecting with Elden Spring Road that had places fairly accessible where a body could easily be taken and concealed," TM said. "We use what's called a hasty search to check out a large area and determine whether there are places where we might want to conduct a more detailed search. Based on the wind direction and the terrain shown on a satellite map, I've mapped out a pattern I'll follow to cover what appears to be the most promising area to find something."

TM left his cell phone in his truck so it wouldn't distract his attention during the search. He kept Jackie on a leash until they reached the starting point of the pattern. He released the leash, gave the dog a treat, and said, "Search."

He then began to walk the pattern as Jackie ran close by. They came to a place where someone had abandoned an old motorcycle and others had stripped it of parts. There were places where someone in a vehicle could easily drive off a dirt road into the forest and find an isolated spot to leave a body. TM was beginning to think the area was so vast and the possible drop sites so numerous that his search was hopeless.

He was about to call Jackie and abandon the search when he saw that she was several yards ahead of him and was in a down stay. He rushed toward her and saw that she had found a body. But unlike the others, it was lying on the ground and in a condition that indicated it had only been there a few days.

TM used the two-way radio Craig had given him and told Craig what he had found and the coordinates shown on his portable GPS.

"Have your people be careful," TM said, "because there could be tire tracks."

As TM waited for the investigators to arrive, he kept his distance from the body but noticed it was a young woman with purple hair. It appeared that her death had been violent and that she had fought hard against her murderer.

When TM arrived back at his truck with Jackie, he turned his cell phone on. Not surprisingly, there was a message from Webster.

I'm in Flagstaff and need to talk to you. Call me as soon as you get this message.

Webster did not mention his phone number, but TM saw it on his cell phone and returned the call.

"Hello?"

"TM. I'm returning your call. We found another body."

"Is that the third?"

"Yes. I can't help you find out whether any of them is your client's daughter unless I get the information about her that I requested. At the very least, I need a good recent photo and a DNA sample."

"I brought both this time. But I need to meet with you because there's been a new development and I don't want to discuss it on the phone."

They agreed to meet in an hour at the hotel where TM was staying.

Webster insisted they go to TM's room to talk.

"My client received a call from a man who said he has kidnapped my client's daughter and wants a ransom. He put the girl on the line, and she confirmed she was being held. But there was a second call, and my client thought the message from his daughter in that call was the same as the message in the first call. He thinks it may have been a recording."

"Did he call the FBI?"

"No. I urged him to, but the kidnapper demanded the police not be called, and my client's wife insisted they comply."

"That's a huge mistake!" TM exclaimed. "Kidnappers always say the police shouldn't be called, but the FBI knows how to deal with the situation. They have incredible resources they can bring to bear to locate the victim and the kidnapper."

"I know. I did my best to try to persuade my client to call the FBI, but he wouldn't listen because of his wife."

"Why have you told me this? I'm just here to do body searches and not to solve kidnappings."

"I guess it's because I feel so desperate. I'm a business lawyer and not a detective. I needed to talk to someone, and because of your background, I felt comfortable confiding in you."

"Why don't you call the FBI?"

"Oh no!" Webster exclaimed. "I promised the client I wouldn't."

"I made no such promise," TM said.

"But it would be the same as if I had broken my promise," Webster cried. "Please, please don't betray my confidence."

TM sat silently for a few moments. "I guess I have two choices then. I can pretend I never heard what you said and go about my business."

Webster's expression changed to one of dismay.

"Or," TM continued, "I can try to help you, which would be a foolish thing for me to do."

"Not at all!" Webster exclaimed. "You could help save a life."

"What did the kidnapper ask for ransom?"

"A million-dollar bearer gold certificate."

Webster then explained what Morgan had said about the availability of bearer gold certificates and his ability to obtain one.

"My client is a very wealthy hedge fund manager," Webster said, "which is why his daughter was the target of the kidnapper."

"The first thing we need to do is find out whether either of the two new bodies is Natalie," TM said. "By the way, was Natalie reported missing to the Flagstaff police?"

"No. But after her parents were unable to reach her, they contacted the university. The people there checked with her teachers and said she had stopped attending classes a couple of weeks before the parents called. They said it was not unusual for students to drop out without telling anyone. At Morgan's request, I came to Flagstaff and tried to find her. I went to where she had been living, but no one there knew her whereabouts."

"Were you able to get into her room?"

"Yes."

"Did it look like her things were still there?

"As far as I could tell."

"Did you find her cell phone?"

"No."

"Did she have any friends?"

"Not that I know of."

"You said you have evidence of Natalie's DNA. What is it?"

"Her father gave me a hairbrush of hers that he found in her room. It has some of her hairs. I have it in a plastic bag in my suitcase."

"DNA samples are supposed to be kept in paper bags, not plastic because plastic bags provide a growth medium for bacteria that can ruin a DNA sample. Give me the brush and photo and I'll give them to the people heading up the investigation," TM said. "If the hair samples haven't been compromised, they should be able to tell me very quickly whether either of the bodies is Natalie. Incidentally, did Natalie have a car?"

"I don't know."

"Do you have her cell phone number?"

"I'm sure I have it somewhere."

"Has anyone checked to see the last time she used her cell phone?"

"I don't think so."

"Did she have her own bank account in Flagstaff?"

"I don't know. Look, I'm a lawyer, not a detective. I did the best I could under the circumstances."

"We need to know a lot more. When was her cell phone last used? When was the last activity with her bank account and any credit cards she had? Can you ask the Morgans for the information needed to answer these questions?"

"No," Webster said. "Our job is not to act as detectives. Our job is to deliver the ransom in exchange for Natalie."

TM sat quietly for a few moments and then said, "I don't feel comfortable taking on that job. As we both know, the FBI should have been contacted because it has the skill and resources to handle a ransom situation. We're both novices in a situation like this and can make it worse. Also there's too much we don't know. When and where was she kidnapped? The assumption is that it happened here in Flagstaff. Is this where she's being held? That seems unlikely to me. Where would the gold certificate be delivered? The kidnapper probably assumes Morgan did contact the FBI and that it would be easier for the bureau to locate and capture him here than in other places having in mind there are not many ways to get out of Flagstaff."

"So what do you suggest?"

"Meet with Morgan and his wife and convince them to call the FBI."

"Knowing them as I do, that won't work."

"Then I'm afraid I can't help you. LE&I is paying for our search work so you can take us off the clock. I'll have Anderson call you with the amount of our charges and wiring instructions. In the meantime, I'll find out whether one of the two additional bodies we found was Natalie's."

"I hope you'll think about it and reconsider. Can I still call you from time to time? I need to be able to talk to someone about this."

"You can call me, but I don't guarantee I'll be at all helpful," TM said.

Webster handed TM the photo and the plastic bag with the hairbrush.

TM looked at the photo and said, "She's a very attractive woman, but she looks a little older than I would have expected. How old is she?"

"She's in her late twenties."

"And still in graduate school?"

"She took some time off after college to travel abroad. I probably shouldn't say this, but her parents have not been happy that she hasn't settled down. Her father got her summer jobs at his investment firm and really wanted her to go to work full time there, but she turned down the opportunity."

"How tall is she, and how much does she weigh?"

"She's about five feet seven and a hundred and twenty pounds. She actually is very attractive."

"I see her hair is blonde. Is that natural?"

"Like so many others', it's not."

"Does she have any unusual markings such as scars, moles, or tattoos?"

"Not that I know of, but obviously I'm not familiar with all the parts of her body."

"Does she have braces or anything unusual about her teeth?"

"Not that I know of."

"OK. I'll let you know what I find out."

9

Craig had set up a command center at a local hotel, where he commandeered all of the meeting rooms. The number of law enforcement agencies had grown, with agents of the Arizona Department of Public Safety and Coconino County Sheriff's Office deputies and deputy coroners now participating in the investigation. Also present were an assistant Coconino County district attorney, an assistant attorney general, and a representative of the Arizona governor's Office. The places where the bodies were found were examined for evidence and photographed by forensic experts from the Department of Public Safety. Even though the bodies were found in a national forest, the FBI was not directly involved, but it was prepared to provide scientific assistance if requested.

TM found Craig in one of the meeting rooms, where he was seated at a large table with two men. He turned toward TM and said, "Have you discontinued the search?"

"No," TM answered. "Jim Anderson is there now and will continue every day until you tell him to stop. But I need to get back to my office in Boulder. I can send someone to replace me, but I think you should be able to get along fine just with Jim."

"When are you leaving?" Craig asked.

"Sometime tomorrow."

"I'd like you to be available for a news conference I'm having tomorrow morning. The press has been all over us implying we're not doing our job because we haven't caught the killer yet. I want to show tomorrow that we're making every effort to find him. It would be helpful if you and Jim could both bring your dogs."

"OK. Have you identified any of the bodies yet? I want to make sure my client's daughter isn't one of them. I brought her photo and a DNA sample."

"We've identified the body you found. Her name is Carol Ryan and she dropped out of the university a few weeks ago but was still living in the campus area."

"It looked to me like she put up quite a fight before she died."

"She did, which was great because we think we retrieved DNA evidence from her fingernails and other places. We haven't identified the other bodies. They were so badly decomposed that the photo you gave me won't help us, but the DNA will. We do know that the first body was an Asian woman, so we'll check out the second body. Let's hope there aren't more."

"While I'm here, I'd like to see if I can find someone who knew my client's daughter and might have some information about her whereabouts."

Craig turned to one of the other men at the table and said, "Charlie here may be able to help you. He's a campus security officer."

Charlie Jameson was a wiry man, about five feet eight inches tall and in his early fifties. He had black hair and what looked like a perpetual smile. "I'll be glad to take you to the administrative offices," he said, smiling. "The people there should be able to help you."

With Jameson's help, TM was able to get a list of the classes Natalie was registered in and the names of her professors. He also learned the address of the place where she was staying when she disappeared. Fortunately one of the classes was scheduled a few minutes later. When it was over, TM met with the professor, a man with a white beard who appeared to be in his fifties. Surprisingly, he was very familiar with Natalie. TM suspected it was because she was so attractive.

"I was very surprised when she stopped coming to class one day," the professor said.

"Did you notice whether she had any close friends in the class?" TM asked.

The professor paused and then said, "Not really. She did chat with some of the others in the class but…wait, there was one girl she seemed to talk with the most."

"What's her name?"

The professor thought for a moment and then said, "Dorothy. Dorothy Westerberg."

"Did Natalie seem depressed or anything before she stopped coming to class?"

"No. She seemed quite happy."

"Thank you very much, Professor."

TM went to the address he had been given for Natalie. It was a two-story frame building that had a few bedrooms, a living room, a kitchen, and two shared bathrooms. The only one there was a young man who said his name was Victor Beshire. He said he hardly knew Natalie and that the people who stayed there didn't spend much time together. He was not even aware Natalie was missing.

The administrative office provided TM with Dorothy Westerberg's address and her cell phone number. She didn't answer when TM called, and he didn't leave a message. He went to her address and found she lived in a large dormitory. He tried her number again, and she answered.

"Hello?" she softly said.

"Dorothy, my name is TM and I'm trying to locate Natalie Morgan. I understand you're a friend of hers."

"Who are you?"

"I'm working with a lawyer who was hired by her family to find Natalie. They are very worried about her. Can I meet with you?"

"I don't know," Dorothy said hesitantly. "I doubt I can help you."

"It's very important, and I won't take much of your time."

"I still don't know. Where would we meet?"

"I'm here in the lobby of your dorm. We could meet here in the living area. Are you nearby?"

"I'm in my room. I'll come down."

Dorothy was a slim, tiny woman just over five feet tall. She had dark, curly hair that needed to be brushed and wore a black blouse and black pants that were unfamiliar with an iron. They found chairs in the corner of the deserted living area.

"I didn't catch your name," Dorothy said. "It sounded like TM."

"That's right," TM said and quickly changed the subject. "I understand you're a good friend of Natalie's."

"I wouldn't say we were great friends, but we did spend time together."

"Did she have a boyfriend?"

"Not here, but sometimes she talked about a male friend of hers that she talked to on her cell phone. They also texted each other."

"Do you know his name?"

"No."

"Did she ever talk about dropping out of school?"

"No. She seemed to like going to school. In fact, this is the fourth college she's attended."

"So you didn't notice anything unusual about her before she disappeared."

"No. She seemed happy. I'll miss her. She was a good friend. She even gave me a scarf of hers that I loved. I often told her how beautiful it was."

"When did she give it to you?"

"The last time I saw her."

"Did she say why she was giving it to you?" "No. She just said, 'I want you to have this.'"

10

Because of the large number of reporters, photographers, and camera crews, the press conference was held in an auditorium at the university. It was carried live on MSNBC, FOX, and CNN, and reporters and cameramen from all the network television stations also covered the conference.

The head of LE&I was not about to let a media opportunity like this pass him by. He opened the conference by thanking the people for attending and gave a brief commercial for LE&I. He then turned the conference over to Craig but stood next to the podium so he would be visible in most of the still and video shots. To deflect any notion that LE&I was not competent to handle the investigation, Craig introduced representatives of all the governmental and other agencies that were assisting in the investigation and invited some of them to talk briefly about their work, including the head of the Arizona Department of Public Safety and the Coconino County sheriff. Both of them said extra police were present in the Flagstaff area to make sure it was safe for residents, visitors, and students.

Craig did not ask TM to speak but praised TM and Anderson for finding two of the bodies. He made a point of having them step forward with Nick and Jackie and with a straight face, took credit for bringing them in to search for the bodies. As Craig had suspected, the photographers and cameramen eagerly pressed to get the best shots of the dogs, and their presence guaranteed the conference would get great coverage on television.

After the introductions and a few comments about how hard everyone was working, Craig said he would take a few questions. The first question was not a surprise.

"Do you have any suspects?"

"Not at this time, but we have recovered significant scientific evidence that is being evaluated at the FBI laboratory and hopefully will lead us to the murderer. In the meantime investigators are pursuing possible leads here in Flagstaff."

"Have you identified the victims?"

"We have identified one of the victims, but we are not prepared to disclose her identity until her parents have been notified."

"Was she a student at the university?"

"No. She was, but she dropped out of school."

TM could see that the questions could go on for a while and left the auditorium through a side door. He went to the parking lot and headed to where Anderson had parked the truck. Suddenly Jackie pulled on the leash TM was holding and attempted to walk in the direction of a line of cars parked a few feet away. TM's first thought was to pull her back and continue toward the truck. Instead, he let her continue and followed behind her. When she came to one of the parked cars, she walked to the rear of the car and dropped to the down position. That meant one thing to TM. Jackie had picked up what she thought was the scent of a cadaver.

"Good girl," TM exclaimed and patted her with approval.

The car was a white Ford Focus, and on both sides of the car in large, black letters were the words *Campus Police.*

11

Craig was about to stop taking questions when he felt his cell phone vibrating and heard the sound of a new text message. He was inclined to ignore it but changed his mind and removed the phone from its case. He looked down and was startled by what he saw.

Urgent. Dog found something major. Call me. TM.

"That's all the time we have for questions," Craig announced. "Thank you for being here."

As the officials and the press started to leave, Craig turned and was about to call TM when the head of LE&I took his arm and said he wanted to review the status of the investigation with him. Craig started to say he had to make a call but was interrupted.

"I have to leave in an hour, so we need to talk now," the LE&I head said.

Frustrated, Craig took his cell phone and pointed to the text message.

"I'm sure it can wait."

"Let me text him back and tell him I'll call him in about an hour."

As soon as Craig had finished the text message, he received a reply.

Call now. I think I know the killer.

TM was standing by the campus police car when Charlie Jameson walked up.

"These dogs of yours are really impressive," Jameson said. "Good work."

"This one has fixed on the rear of your car," TM said. "Could you please open the trunk?"

"It probably smells some old sandwiches I left there a couple of weeks ago. I'm late for patrol and have to get going."

"I'm afraid that won't work. Craig should be here soon, and I suggest you wait until he comes."

"I don't need to wait for anyone. You're not law enforcement, and I don't have to pay any attention to what you say. You're on university property and I'm law enforcement here, so get out of the way."

Jameson entered the car and quickly drove away just as Anderson and Nick came to the parking lot. TM briefed Anderson on what had just happened.

"I hated to see him drive off," TM said, "but there was nothing I could do. He was right. I'm not a law enforcement officer, and at least where we are now, he is. It's too bad Craig couldn't break away and come here when I texted him."

"We might as well go back to the hotel," Anderson said. "The dogs need to be walked to do their business, and it's feeding time."

It was a couple of hours later before Craig called TM.

"I'm sorry it took so long for me to get back to you. You have no idea what I've had to go through with the head of LE&I. He was more concerned with getting the right publicity than with solving the murders. Your texts were astonishing. Tell me what you found."

"As I came out of the auditorium with my dog, Jackie, and was walking in the parking lot, Jackie suddenly veered toward a parked vehicle and assumed the position that tells me there were indications of a cadaver. The vehicle was a campus police car. Just then Charlie Jameson walked up. I asked him to open the trunk, but he refused. He then got in and drove away."

"That's it?" Craig asked. "Your texts were so emphatic about finding the killer, but I expected more."

"I trust our dogs," TM said. "If she signaled cadaver scent, there was something there."

"Did your other dog also signal cadaver scent?" "No. Anderson came after Jameson had left."

"Let's do this," Craig said. "I'll arrange for Jameson to bring the vehicle some place where we can investigate further. I won't indicate in any way that he's under suspicion. Can we wait until morning?"

"It would be better to do it now, but we can live with waiting until tomorrow."

Craig called TM in the morning and said he had asked Jameson to come to Craig's office at ten to discuss how they should proceed.

"Have Anderson bring your other dog, but make sure Jameson won't know what you're doing," Craig said.

TM and Anderson arrived at Craig's office at nine thirty and made sure they parked the truck where Jameson could not see it. Jameson was right on time. He parked the patrol car at ten and entered the building. TM and Anderson waited a few minutes and then took Nick out of the truck and walked toward the patrol car.

"Is that the same car?" Anderson asked.

"Yes," TM replied. "I recognize the license number. It's XT nine-four-five and is a government plate."

Anderson led Nick in a straight line about ten feet parallel to the rear of the car. The dog moved straight ahead and made no motion when it was abreast of the car. Anderson walked farther and then turned and led Nick on a straight line closer to the car. Nick walked right by. Finally Anderson led Nick directly to the back of the car. The dog sat and looked at Anderson as though expecting some command.

"Let's go," TM said. "He obviously doesn't pick up a cadaver scent."

"What did you find?" Craig asked when he met with TM and Anderson several minutes later. "Did your other dog pick up the same scent?"

"No," TM said.

"Could he have gotten rid of the scent between yesterday and today?"

"It's possible," TM said. "But not likely. He would have had to use a tremendous amount of detergent and chemicals, and even then some cadaver scent would remain."

"So your dog was wrong. Thank goodness I wasn't able to respond when you texted me. We could have had serious problems if we had confronted him and accused him of being the killer. A lawsuit for sure, and it probably would have cost me my job."

"I'm still not convinced," TM said.

He handed Craig a piece of paper.

"While Anderson was working the dog, I looked in the front windshield and wrote down the vehicle identification number. I also wrote down the license plate number. You should have ADOT check to see if they match."

"You don't give up easily," Craig said. "Do you."

"Will you check it out or should I do it?" TM said.

"I wouldn't push me, if I were you."

With that, TM grabbed the paper from Craig's hand, turned, and walked toward the truck, with Anderson and Nick right behind.

"Oh, by the way," Craig said. "I'm terminating your contract. We're bringing in some dogs from another Forest Service location."

TM remembered that Rick Meyer, the head of the Arizona Department of Public Safety, had been present at the press briefing. They had chatted before the briefing, and Meyer had been very interested in the dogs. TM did not have Meyer's direct number, and trying to get through the various layers of officials at DPS was challenging. Finally TM was able to talk to Meyer's executive assistant.

"I was with Mr. Meyer in Flagstaff at the press conference about the serial killer," TM said. "My dogs were the ones that discovered the bodies, and I'm sure Mr. Meyer will remember me."

"Hello?" a voice said.

"Mr. Meyer?"

"Yes?"

"This is TM. Our dogs found the bodies, and you and I chatted about it before the press conference."

"Of course. What can I do for you?"

"I think we found something that can help us locate the killer."

"Why are you calling me? Aren't you working with the local law enforcement officials in Flagstaff?"

"I have been, but the people I've been working with are questioning our dogs' effectiveness. As you mentioned to me, your department has dogs that assist your people in investigative matters and you have a high regard for them. I'm not asking you to take sides but only to help me get the facts to determine who's right."

"What do you want me to do?"

"Let me meet with one of your lead investigators and give him the details. He can listen and decide whether it's worth pursuing."

"OK. Are you still in Flagstaff?"

"Yes. It would be great if your person could meet me tomorrow."

"I'll send Carson Cooper. Where and when will you meet?"

"The lobby of the Flagstaff Radisson at one."

12

It was the same muffled voice Morgan had heard when he answered the phone in his home office midafternoon.

"Do you have the bearer bond?" the voice asked.

"No," Morgan exclaimed. "I'm working on it, but it takes time."

"When will you have it?"

"Probably next week."

"I think you're stalling," the voice shouted.

"No. No. But I need to know Natalie's still alive. The last voice of hers I heard sounded like a recording of the first time I heard her. Put her on the phone now."

"Don't you tell me what to do!"

"I need to know she's still alive."

"I'll call you back in an hour," the muffled voice said and hung up.

It was over two hours later when the phone rang.

"I'll put her on the line," the muffled voice said.

"Daddy. It's Natalie," she exclaimed.

"Are you all right?" Morgan shouted.

"Yes. But I'm scared and miss you and Mom. Tell her I love her and—"

"That's enough," the muffled voice said. "I expect you to have the bearer bond when I call you early next week. And don't call the police."

With that, he hung up.

"We can definitely stop the search now," Morgan said to Webster.

"What happened?" Webster asked.

"The kidnapper called and put Natalie on the phone. I was able to ask her a question, and she answered."

"That's a huge relief. What happens now? Did he tell you where to deliver the bond?"

"No. He was irritated that I don't have it yet. He said he would call back early next week."

"Will you have it then?"

"I should have it tomorrow."

13

TM arrived at the Radisson lobby at 12:45 p.m. It was very spacious and had a large seating area with several chairs and small tables. The lobby was deserted except for the desk clerks and a man who appeared to be the concierge. At exactly 1:00 p.m. TM saw someone enter the lobby from a side door. The person turned out to be a trim woman about five feet eight who wore her dark hair in a bun. She was wearing jeans, a blue open-necked shirt, a black jacket, and wire-rimmed glasses. Her face was pale without makeup, and it was difficult to tell her age. She wore a red backpack that led TM to think she was a student. But when she saw TM, she walked toward him.

"Are you the dog man?" she asked when she was just a few feet away.

"That's one way to put it," TM said. "Are you Carson Cooper?"

"Yes," she said. "I only had the initials TM and didn't know your name."

"That is my name."

She paused and gave him a long look that combined disbelief with disapproval. "Whatever," she finally said. "What's so important you wanted to tell us?"

TM pointed to a corner area of the lobby and said, "Let's go sit down where we can talk without being overheard."

When they were seated, TM explained what had taken place in the auditorium parking lot and the subsequent failure of Nick to signal a cadaver scent at the rear of what appeared to be the same vehicle Jackie had highlighted.

"The two vehicles had the same license plate," TM said. "I wrote down the vehicle identification number of the second vehicle, and it needs to be checked to make sure it matches the license number."

"What makes you think it doesn't?" Cooper said.

"I have great confidence in our dogs. Jackie was as positive about her scent stance as I've ever seen."

"But to have me come here just to determine if there is a match doesn't make much sense. The records are with the Department of Transportation and not our department. Couldn't you have contacted the ADOT people yourself?"

"I'm not a law enforcement person, and the information isn't publicly available. And the person from the Forest Service heading up the kidnapping investigation wouldn't help me. If I'm right that there's not a match, your department, DPS, rather than ADOT, would be the one to follow up."

"OK. Let me see if there's Wi-Fi here."

She opened her backpack and took out a laptop. "There is," she said. "Let's hope it's free. We have a direct link to ADOT's records."

TM handed her the paper with the license number and the vehicle identification number. She was silent for a few moments as she worked the keyboard.

"They don't match," she said. "The license plate number and the ID number are both for a 2010 Ford Focus. It looks like the university has three 2010 Ford Focuses that were licensed at the same time. It could be they got the license plates mixed up and placed them on the wrong cars."

She took out a pad from her backpack and wrote down several numbers. "Someone needs to look at the three cars and get the license plate and ID numbers of all three," she said. "It would be interesting to see which vehicle matched the license plate number and which matches the ID number."

"Who would that someone be?" TM asked. "I nominate you."

"I didn't expect to be here overnight, but given the fact that my boss seems to like you, I guess I'd better stay. It shouldn't be that difficult for me to track down the three cars and get the information."

"I don't think you'll have any trouble doing that."

"Why do you say that?"

"I don't think anyone would suspect you're a police investigator."

"I don't think that's a compliment. Here's my card. Call me tomorrow afternoon and I'll tell you what I've learned."

The call from Webster was short and direct.

"We have satisfied ourselves that Natalie is still alive, so I was told to terminate your services. But I would still like to confide in you from time to time."

"Well, we've been fired by both clients," TM said to Anderson. "So you better head back to Boulder. I'm working with an investigator from the Arizona Department of Safety to see if we can trace the DNA to Jameson."

"How did you find him?" Anderson asked.

"It's a her and not a him. Her name is Carson Cooper, and the head of DPS who was at the press conference assigned her to work on this."

"Good luck."

"Thanks, I'll need it."

"I located two of the cars," Cooper said when TM called her the next day. "One of them has the numbers you wrote down that don't match. The other has numbers that do match."

"What about the third car?" TM asked.

"I couldn't find it. But I was able to talk to a man in university administration who said that because of budget cuts, the university reduced the patrol staff and only uses two cars."

"Did you have to identify yourself?"

"Of course not. People have a way of telling you things if you talk to them in the right way."

"Did the person tell you where the other car is?"

"No. He didn't know."

"Great," TM said. "Why don't you just identify yourself and ask someone in authority where the car is?"

"You can't be serious?"

"No. But no harm in asking."

"As soon as I identified myself and started to ask questions, all hell would break loose. They would call their counsel and demand to know why I was asking questions. Then they would call my boss, who would be furious and probably fire me."

"Oh. Sorry I asked."

"The only thing I can think of is for me to tell my boss everything and ask him whether we can investigate. But I doubt he'll approve.

We're not the lead in the kidnapping investigation so he would have to try and clear it first with the Forest Service person who already dissed you."

"There's one other way," TM said. "They were able to retrieve DNA evidence from the last victim. If we could get a DNA sample from Jameson, we could rule him in or out right away."

"Why didn't you tell me there was DNA evidence? The DNA test was either done by our crime lab or the FBI lab. If the FBI lab did it, I'm sure it would share the information with our lab. Who is Jameson?"

"He's the campus patrol officer who had the car that my dog identified as having the cadaver scent. I'm sorry I didn't mention his name before. How do we get a DNA sample from him?"

"I can get one," Cooper said. "But it may take me a few days. Give me your cell phone number and I'll call you when I have it."

"But you don't know what Jameson looks like. The last thing we need is to get a DNA sample from the wrong guy. I better go with you and identify him for you. Also, if I'm right, this guy's a killer. We don't need you to be the next victim."

"OK. I need you to identify him. But after that I work alone. I don't intend to have an altercation with him, but if something happens, I can take care of myself."

TM and Cooper drove in Cooper's car to the parking lot next to the university's main administration building, and Cooper parked the car where they could see people coming and going from the entrance. Cooper opened her backpack and took out binoculars. They waited in silence for a few minutes until TM finally spoke.

"How will you get a DNA sample?"

"I'll follow him and look for something that could have his DNA on it. It doesn't take much. Anything that has a few cells on it, like a toothpick, a cigarette butt, a tissue, or a cup or glass that he drank out of. If I'm in luck, he's a spitter and I can collect some of that. I don't expect to get a sample that would convict him in a court, but I should get enough to obtain a preliminary match with the sample from the killer so he can be taken into custody for more extensive DNA collection. But I'll still take precautions. I'll wear gloves when I take samples and put them in paper bags I brought with me. How will you know Jameson when you see him?"

"He's thin, about five feet eight, and has black hair. He always seems to be smiling, even when I confronted him in the parking lot."

They waited in silence until dusk with no sign of Jameson.

"Are you sure he comes here?" Cooper asked.

"Reasonably sure," TM said. "Let's come back early tomorrow. Do you live in Flagstaff?"

"No."

"Where are you staying?

"At a cheap motel on old Highway 66. It's all I could afford with my per diem. Fortunately I had extra clothes in my car. I learned to do that the hard way."

"Let me help you with your per diem."

"How's that?"

"I'll buy you dinner."

"No. I'd better not do that."

"OK. But I'd appreciate it if you would give me a ride to my hotel because my assistant has the truck."

Cooper picked TM up at his hotel at daybreak the next morning, and they went back to the same spot in the parking lot. They were there for only a few minutes when a white university patrol car pulled up in front of the administration building entrance.

"That's him," TM said when a man came out of the car and walked toward the entrance.

Cooper immediately lifted the binoculars and followed the man until he entered the building.

"OK," Cooper said. "Now I'll do my thing."

14

"You have the bond, right?" the muffled voice said.

"It was difficult, but I have it," Morgan replied.

"Listen carefully to my instructions. You will need to write them down."

"OK. I have pen and paper."

"You will send the bond by air courier to Rafael Ulate, care of Rand Trading Company at three-twenty-three Avenida Four, San Jose, Costa Rica. The telephone number from the United States is 011 506 9993 7658."

"How do I get Natalie?"

"Rafael Ulate is strictly an intermediary. He knows nothing about Natalie's situation. He will examine the bond to make sure it is legitimate. If he finds that it is, he will give you information that will enable you to locate Natalie."

"How soon after do I get the information?"

"Very soon."

"Is she in Costa Rica?"

"Yes."

"When will the transfer take place?"

"A week from Friday."

"I don't like the idea of sending the bond to the intermediary in advance, particularly when I don't know anything about him. We'll deliver the bond to him in person and wait while he authenticates it."

"That may not be possible. And what do you mean by we? It should be you."

"No. I'm too emotionally involved. I would send someone."

"Who?"

"My lawyer."

"What's his name?"

"Daniel Webster."

"You're making this too complicated. I'll call you tomorrow," the muffled voice said and hung up.

"This is ridiculous," Webster said after Morgan called him and related the phone conversation. "It's hard to believe Natalie would be in Costa Rica. How could the kidnapper get her there without her having the opportunity to seek help from someone at an immigration booth, an airport, a train station, or some other public place? I wonder whether she even had a passport with her."

"I don't know," Morgan said. "When he calls back tomorrow, I'll ask him. But I'm not sure we have any choice but to do as he says. Can I count on you to deliver the bond and get Natalie?"

There was silence, and then Webster said, "I'm not up to it, Jeff. I'm in my sixties, and I don't think I can handle the stress this would entail. It also could be very dangerous."

"What will we do then?" Morgan shouted. "I can't see myself doing it either."

There was a long silence.

"TM," Webster said.

"What?" Morgan shouted. "We can't talk about this situation with anyone else."

"I already told him about the kidnapping," Webster said. "And I trust him not to tell anyone else."

"What makes you think he'd do it?"

"I'm not sure he will, but he'd be good for the job and I can't think of anyone else."

"But what would we tell the kidnapper? That TM is you?"

"That's a possibility, but it could be risky. He would have to have a passport to enter the country and some identification to book flights and a hotel room. If the kidnapper found out TM wasn't me, he would probably think TM is some kind of police officer and abort the transfer."

"It doesn't help matters that his name is TM," Morgan said.

"I know. We'll just have to live with that."

"Who do we tell the kidnapper TM is?"

"We'll have to think of something. But we have one good thing going for us."

"What's that?"

"The kidnapper wants one million dollars, and we're the only ones who can get it for him."

Morgan was ready when the muffled voice called the next day and had Webster listening on an extension phone. "I'm not comfortable with what you told me," Morgan said. "I can't understand how Natalie could be in Costa Rica. She would have had to go through several checkpoints where she could have gotten someone to help her escape from you."

"We did not come here by public means," the muffled voice said. "We came by private plane. It's much easier to fly out of the States than it is to fly in."

"I can't take your word for it. Put Natalie on the phone and have her tell me she's in Costa Rica."

"You're making this difficult," the muffled voice said. "Hold on."

A few minutes passed.

"Daddy, Daddy," Natalie cried. "I want to come home."

"Where are you?" Morgan asked.

"In San Jose."

"How did you get there?" Morgan asked.

"Enough," the muffled voice shouted. "She answered your question. Let's get down to business. When will you send the bond?"

"There's one other thing."

"What's that?"

"I can't come and neither can my lawyer. We have to send someone else."

"Impossible," the muffled voice shouted.

"Just a minute," Morgan shouted back. "I told you I couldn't come. My lawyer is in his sixties and is unable to travel out of the country. We have no choice but to send someone else. We want Natalie, and you want the million-dollar bond. There has to be a way of doing this that works for both of us."

"Who would you send?"

"A man who has worked with us and is completely reliable and discrete. He has a business that provides personal security protection for wealthy people. He protects them and doesn't ask questions. We would send him and not one of his employees."

"What's his name?"

"Everybody calls him TM."

"Is that his name?"

"I don't know. I just know him as TM."

"When can he come?"

"I don't have a firm date from him," Morgan said. "Call me back in three days and I'll give you a date."

"It sounds like you're stalling and up to something. My next call will be the last," the muffled voice said and hung up.

"Are you sure TM will do it?" Morgan asked Webster.

"He has to do it," Webster said. "But it probably will cost you a lot of money."

15

TM was in his hotel room in the late afternoon when his cell phone rang.

"I think I have what we need," Cooper said. "It wasn't easy, but I have two samples that should provide an answer."

"Great," TM said. "Where are you now?"

"I just pulled into the parking lot at my motel and…wait! Oh my God…"

"Cooper. Cooper. What's happening?" TM shouted.

The line went dead.

I need to find her, TM thought. *But I don't know where she is. Only that it's a motel on 66.*

He ran from his room to the hotel parking lot and drove his rental car to the stretch of Highway 89 that was called old Highway 66. He turned left and headed toward the main part of Flagstaff. There were no buildings on the left side of the road because of a railroad track. He soon came to the beginning of the strip of old motels. But there were several of them, and he didn't know which one was hers. He moved to the right side of the road and drove slowly so he could see the parking lots. Impatient drivers behind him honked their horns, but he didn't care. Something caught his eye coming from the opposite direction. It was a white university patrol car.

The campus is in the opposite direction, he said to himself. *Where is he going?*

He continued driving and passed motels with nothing unusual in the parking lots and was beginning to think he had missed Cooper's motel. But then he saw something else that caught his attention. There in a motel parking lot was a car with the driver's side door open. He had already passed the entrance, so he drove to the next cross street, turned right, and found a place where he could turn around and return to the motel.

When he pulled in behind the car with the open door, he saw it was the same model and color as the one Cooper had been driving. He jumped out of his car and looked inside the other car. There was no one inside, but the key was still in the ignition, and he saw the special DPS radio and other equipment. *The patrol car I saw heading north must be involved,* he thought. But catching up with it would be difficult. He thought he had an answer.

He parked his rental car in an open space and went back to Cooper's car. He started the motor and quickly moved into the lanes headed north. The car was faster and more responsive than his rental car, and he was hopeful it had emergency flashing lights and maybe even a siren.

Fortunately traffic was light, and he was able to move at a rapid pace but still not as fast as he would have liked. It was difficult to work the extra controls he saw while he kept his eyes on the road. He felt for a switch and triggered it, but it only illuminated a small computer monitor. The next switch was more helpful because he could see in the reflections before him that he had activated the flashing lights. But the traffic became more congested and the flashing lights were useless because the cars several lengths ahead couldn't see them. He groped the other controls without success until he located a small lever on the steering column. He pulled it toward him and immediately heard the welcoming sound of a siren. By moving the lever in different directions, he was able to change the sound from the familiar whining siren to the impatient siren used when the way ahead was blocked.

He was now able to drive ahead rapidly, but there was a new dilemma. Which way should he go? He could drive straight on Highway 89 headed out of Flagstaff toward Elden Spring Road, or he could turn right at the next intersection and have more choices—whether to head east on Interstate 40, west on Interstate 40, or straight on University Drive.

He decided to continue on Highway 89 because that would bring him to the side roads of the Coconino National Forest more quickly. He passed the Flagstaff Mall and in minutes was past the last signal light as the speed limit increased to fifty-five miles an hour. There was little traffic so he turned off the siren and the emergency flashing lights but still drove several miles higher than the speed limit.

Before long he saw a white car ahead of him in the distance. As he drew closer, he could see that it was the university patrol car. He reduced his speed so he could stay several car lengths behind. It was growing dark, but he turned off the automatic headlight switch. There were no lights on the patrol car either. But he soon saw the patrol car's brake lights as it reduced speed and then turned right onto a dirt road.

TM slowed his car and followed. It was dark now, and he could barely see the patrol car in front of him. Then the patrol car stopped. TM drove to within thirty feet of it and stopped as well.

TM was not armed, and no weapon was evident in Cooper's car. He was sure Jameson was the driver of the patrol car. Jameson had not been armed when TM had seen him in the auditorium parking lot or when TM and Cooper had seen him later. *But he could have a weapon in his car,* TM thought.

Minutes passed, and no one came out of the patrol car. *If he has Cooper,* TM thought, *I have to make a move.* He stepped out of his car and started walking toward the patrol car.

He had gone only a few feet when the driver's door of the patrol car opened. Jameson stepped out and immediately rushed toward TM. In his right hand he carried a billy stick made of Arizona ironwood. As he came closer, Jameson raised the billy stick and swung it at TM's head.

At the last moment, TM leapt to his left, pivoted on his right foot, and grabbed Jameson from behind in a bear hug with his arms around Jameson's arms. Jameson braced himself, pushed back, and knocked TM backward on the ground. TM still had his arms around Jameson, but as they rolled to one side, Jameson was able to free himself. Jameson still held the billy stick, but before he could strike TM, TM swung the blade of his right hand into Jameson's nose. There was a crunch of small bones breaking, and spurting blood temporarily blinded both of them. Jameson swung the billy stick, but it just grazed TM's head above his left ear.

As they both were getting to their feet, Jameson brought his right knee up and caught TM under his chin. Jameson raised the billy stick to smash TM in the head. But as the billy stick started to descend, two hands grabbed it. The hands wrenched the billy stick out of Jameson's grasp and brought it to his neck. As Jameson reached up to release the pressure on his neck, a dazed TM rose and drove his fist into Jameson's stomach. The hands increased the pressure on Jameson's neck until he was unconscious.

"Cooper!" TM shouted. "Where did you—"

"Let's get him under control first," she said.

She opened the trunk of her car, retrieved handcuffs, and securely placed them on Jameson's hands. She then reached inside her car and took out her cell phone. She noted the coordinates of their position, dialed a number, and spoke a code.

"He Tasered me," Cooper said. "He opened the door when I was talking to you and I felt this terrible shock. Then he pulled me out of my car and stuffed me into the trunk of his car. When he stopped the car, I was afraid he would Taser me again and kill me. But when I heard the commotion of the two of you fighting, I found the cord that released the trunk and jumped out. You know the rest. How are you?"

"I may have some loose teeth and my head hurts where he hit me on the side of it," TM said. "But thanks to you, I'm still alive."

"You certainly saved my life as well."

They could hear sirens in the distance, and soon a highway patrol car pulled up behind them. In a few minutes, two other highway patrol cars joined them and a police helicopter hovered above. Jameson was starting to regain consciousness and was placed in the back of one of the cars.

"We'll need a complete report from both of you," one of the officers said. "But in your present state it's best to do that tomorrow. We need to keep Agent Cooper's car here while we process the evidence, so one of us will drive you back to town."

The highway patrol car took TM and Cooper to the motel where Cooper was staying. Neither one had much to say during the ride. TM retrieved his rental car and drove back to his hotel.

When he reached his room, he noticed that he had both a voice mail and a text message from Webster. They said the same thing: "Where are you? It's urgent for me to talk to you."

Tomorrow, TM said to himself, and went to bed.

17

TM was awakened the next morning by a phone call from the hotel's front desk.

"There's a policeman here to see you."

"What time is it?" TM asked.

"Seven thirty."

"Tell him I'll be down in a few minutes."

He shaved, showered, and somewhat painfully put on his clothes. When he reached the small lobby, he saw a young uniformed officer.

"I'm Officer Timothy Murphy, and I'm here to give you a ride to our local headquarters to go over the events of last night."

"OK. But I'd like to get some breakfast first."

"I'm sorry, but my orders are to bring you to headquarters right away."

"If that means you'll arrest me if I have breakfast, go ahead. Otherwise you're welcome to join me."

Obviously uncomfortable, Officer Murphy said, "I'm just following orders, but I guess we have time for breakfast if you don't take too long."

Thirty minutes later, Officer Murphy drove TM to the local DPS headquarters. TM was surprised to see that Cooper was there and that she clearly wasn't happy.

"You won't believe this," she said, "but we're under investigation for what we did last night."

"You've got to be kidding," TM said. "What's going on?"

"Jameson is claiming we assaulted him and wants us arrested on several charges, including attempting to murder a law enforcement official."

"But he went after you and put you in the trunk of his car."

"He said he did that because he saw me take something out of his car."

"Did you?"

"I saw a tissue on the front seat of his car and I opened the door and took it for a DNA sample. I didn't think anyone saw me, and surely not him."

"But why would he put you in the trunk of his car?"

"He said he did it because he didn't have prisoner restraints in his vehicle."

"But why would he head out of town instead of to the nearest police station?"

"He said he was going to, but he saw you following him and was trying to get away from you."

"That's nonsense. I saw him headed out of town before I found you."

"That's not what he says."

"He's lying, of course. What about the DNA samples? Did they take additional samples from him last night?"

"I don't think so. He came in here so belligerent that people were intimidated by him."

"Is there anything we can do?"

"I called my boss and told him everything. Fortunately he has confidence in me and still likes you because of the dogs. He said he would have his people run the DNA samples I took and also have them look for the other patrol car."

"What happens now?"

"He talked the county attorney into holding off charging us with anything for twenty-four hours. So we're free to leave here, but we have to stay in Flagstaff and be available to return here on short notice."

"How long will it take to evaluate the DNA samples and determine if there's a match?"

"The samples have been rushed to our lab, and if we're lucky, it could only take a few days."

"With our luck, it will take longer," TM said.

TM was able to get Officer Murphy to drive him back to his hotel. When he was in his room, he noticed that he had another text and voice mail from Webster. In both, Webster sounded desperate. TM decided to return the calls.

"Hello?" Webster said.

"It's TM."

"Thank God. I need to meet with you. Are you still in Flagstaff?"

"Yes."

"I'll be there in the morning."

"Can't we talk on the phone?

"No. We need your help and will make it very worthwhile for you."

He hung up.

TM was on the treadmill in the hotel's fitness room when his cell phone rang. It was Cooper.

"Good news," Cooper said. "They found the missing patrol car. It was near the place where we had the encounter with Jameson. Someone had spray painted the sides so you couldn't see the wording. The vehicle ID matches the license plate you first saw in the auditorium parking lot."

"Great," TM replied. "We can get both dogs to fix on the trunk."

"Not necessary. They found signs of human fluids and are sending samples to the lab. They're taking Jameson into custody, and we've been released from restrictions and are free to go wherever we want. I'm leaving tomorrow morning."

"Oh. So am I. But with all you've been through, you deserve a nicer dinner than your per diem would cover."

"What do you have in mind?"

"The country club has a public dining room. We could have dinner there."

After a pause, Cooper said, "I don't know. Where is it?"

"It's not far from my hotel. You could pick me up, and we can go there together."

Another pause.

"What time?" Cooper asked.

"Come by at seven."

"OK, I guess," Cooper slowly said.

TM was standing in front of his hotel when, precisely at seven, Cooper's car pulled up. She said nothing as he sat down in the passenger's seat and she drove away. He turned and was startled by what he saw. The bun was gone, and her silky black hair flowed to her shoulders. Also gone were her wire-rimmed glasses. Although she was seated, her revealing outfit unmasked her beauty. He gave her the directions to the country club but otherwise said nothing. As they were led to a table in the dining room, the eyes of the other dinner guests, both men and women, followed her.

They sat silently across from each other until TM finally found words to say. "You look great, Cooper."

"Thank you," she said quietly.

"I'm going to have a glass of Chardonnay. What would you like?"

"I'd like that too."

TM ordered a bottle of Kendall Jackson and after they studied the menu, gave the waitress their selections.

"Carson Cooper is an unusual name," TM said. "Why did you parents name you that?"

She gave him a look of displeasure but then smiled. "You're the last person to talk about unusual names. Why is your name just TM?" Cooper asked.

"I only explain that to my good friends," TM said.

"Oh," Cooper said with a pout.

"But you're a good friend," TM said with a smile.

"Please," Cooper said.

"I was dropped off at the county orphanage when I was an infant. The people there thought I was so difficult that they called me The Monster. After a while it just became TM. They wanted to get back at me so they persuaded the local county clerk, who wasn't too bright, to issue my birth certificate with TM as the name."

"Why didn't you get it changed when you got older?" Cooper asked.

"I got so used to being TM that I didn't think of changing. And maybe part of me enjoyed the confusion it created whenever my name came up in various situations."

"Did people still call you The Monster?"

"No," TM said, blushing. "Some people called me The Man."

"How egotistical," Cooper said.

"I never suggested or encouraged that," TM said with a hurt look on his face.

"I'm sorry," Cooper said. "I'm sure you gave people good reasons to call you The Man. I noticed you have a slight limp. Why?"

"Shortly after nine/eleven, I was part of a Ranger force that fought in Afghanistan. We were involved in a major firefight, and I was seriously wounded. It took weeks, but thanks to great health care from the army, I was able to recover fully except for the slight limp. But you didn't answer my question. Why did your parents name you Carson Cooper?"

"My mother wanted a daughter, and my father wanted a son. It sounds stupid, but they named me Carson so he could have a son."

"What do your friends call you?"

"CC."

"I knew we had something in common. We're both initials."

"That's pretty corny," she said.

"How did you become an investigator?"

"I went to the University of Arizona and got a bachelor's degree in public administration with a criminal justice major and then took online courses to get a master's degree in criminology. I've been with DPS for four years."

"Do you like it?"

"Yes. But I'd like to move on to something else."

"What?"

"Maybe the FBI. I've been taking accounting courses online so I can possibly qualify for a position as a financial investigator."

"Do you live by yourself?"

"That's none of your business," she exclaimed. "But to answer your real question, I'm not married. How did you start working with dogs?"

"When I was in Afghanistan, I witnessed an Australian Special Forces unit that had a dog trained to detect explosives. I was very impressed with what they did and decided to train dogs for various skills, including, of course, cadaver detection."

"Where is your business located?"

"Just outside Boulder, Colorado."

"Is dog training your only business?"

"No. I also have a personal protection business that provides private security personnel for high-profile business executives, sports figures, entertainers, and others. From time to time I also do private contract work for federal agencies."

"Are you a spy?" she asked, laughing.

"No. I've done a number of different things, including working under cover, but I've never been a spy."

"I won't ask you if you live alone," she said.

"You just did, and the answer is I'm not married either."

The waitress brought their dinner, and they ate in silence until one of them said what was on both their minds.

"We both came close to the end," she said.

"I know," he said and reached across to hold her hand.

"I'll never forget what happened," she said, "and I'll never forget you."

He paid the check and took her hand as they left the building. When they reached his hotel, she pulled up to the entrance and they sat in silence.

"We can't leave each other like this," he said.

She nodded and drove the car to a parking space. Soon they were in his room and holding each other closely. She pulled back and lifted her dress over her head as he undid his clothes. They kissed each other recklessly as the stress of their experience began to ease. And then they were joined together in a passionate coupling that reached a climatic ecstasy. Exhausted, they laid back and fell into the deepest sleep they had known in days.

18

When TM woke up the next morning, Cooper was gone. He found a note on the desk written on the hotel's memo paper.

TM

I hope you will not forget me.
I will also remember you.

Love, CC

He stared at the note for a few minutes and then folded it and put it in a pocket of his traveling bag. After he shaved and showered, he grabbed his cell phone. He had turned it off before he went to dinner with Cooper, and he was soon glad he had. When he turned it on, there were several frantic text messages and voice mails from Webster. He hesitated and then called Webster.

"TM?" Webster cried when he answered. "It's urgent that I talk to you. Where are you?"

TM gave him the address of the hotel and said he would be in the dining room having breakfast. He was just finishing when Webster arrived.

"We need a quiet place to talk," Webster said. "Can we go to your room?"

"No," TM quickly answered. "Let's go outside. There's a seating area at the side of the hotel. What's so important?"

"The kidnapper has set a place for Natalie to be exchanged for the gold bearer bond, and we need your help."

"I told you I'm not comfortable being involved. You should have called the FBI."

"Of course," Webster said. "But Natalie's parents wouldn't let us, and now you could be the difference between her life or death."

"That's outrageous!" TM exclaimed.

"It sounds outrageous, but it's true. The kidnapper took Natalie to Costa Rica, and that's where the exchange will take place. We have no one else to turn to for the exchange except you."

"Nonsense. What about her father? What about you?"

"Her father's too emotionally devastated, and look at me. I'm in my late sixties, my health isn't that good, and there is no way I could handle this."

"You could get someone else."

"There's no time. You're the only person other than the family and me who knows about the kidnapping. The kidnapper has set a deadline for us to get back to him by tomorrow."

"But Costa Rica? How could the kidnapper get her down there?"

"We wondered about that too and asked him about that. He said they flew there in a private plane."

"I find that hard to believe."

"But the kidnapper put Natalie on the phone, and she said she was in Costa Rica."

"Are you sure this isn't a scam and Natalie's part of it?"

"Absolutely not. She loves her parents and would never do anything to hurt them."

"You're sure?"

"I'm insulted you would question this."

"So what would you want me to do?"

"You would fly to San Jose with the bearer bond and exchange it for Natalie. It wouldn't be that complicated."

"Wrong. It probably would be illegal for me to leave the country with the bearer bond."

"Well, we could send it to you in San Jose by courier."

"What are the arrangements for the exchange?"

"The kidnapper has found an intermediary who will verify the authenticity of the bearer bond and give you the information to locate Natalie."

"Do you really believe this so-called intermediary isn't working with the kidnapper?"

"The kidnapper says the intermediary doesn't know anything about Natalie's situation. Look, TM, it's not an ideal situation, but what choice do we have? Natalie told her father she was in San Jose and sounded frightened."

"What would I be paid for doing this?"

"Five thousand dollars plus expenses."

TM sat silent for a few minutes.

"I see plenty of things that could go wrong," he said. "And it would not be without considerable risk for me. I would need a fee of twenty-five thousand dollars plus an advance of ten thousand dollars toward my expenses. The total would have to be wired to my bank before I would leave."

Webster hesitated and then said, "OK. It's too much money, but we don't have much choice. When can you leave?"

"I have to get back to my place in Boulder and attend to a few things. It'll take a day to get there, and then I want two days to check out the situation before I meet with the intermediary."

"But he gave us a deadline of Thursday," Webster exclaimed.

"That's the best I can do. Thursday's only three days from now, and that's too soon. Tell him I'll meet him on Saturday. I'll leave this afternoon for Boulder. Call me if you want to proceed. But the money would have to be in my bank by the close of business tomorrow."

Before he left, TM went to the county attorney's office and was able to persuade him that, with all the DNA evidence they had, the billy stick was no longer important to the case that would be presented against Jameson.

"It almost cost me my life, and I'd like to keep it as a reminder of how fortunate I was," TM said.

Against his better judgment, the county attorney released it to TM.

19

"That's too late," Morgan cried. "The kidnapper wants it done Thursday. And thirty-five thousand dollars is ridiculous. How could he possibly have that much in expenses? The airplane tickets can't cost all that much, and he'll only be staying in San Jose for a couple of days."

"I thought he would want more than twenty-five thousand," Webster replied. "We'll just have to tell the kidnapper that Saturday is the earliest TM can make it. Remember, he wants a million dollars, and we're the only ones who will give it to him."

"I really hate to send the bearer bond by courier, but I guess we have no choice. Where will he be staying?"

"I've made a reservation for him at the Crowne Plaza. I'll give your secretary the address and phone number. I'll also give her wiring instructions for sending the money to TM's bank."

"So tomorrow we send off a million thirty-five thousand dollars and can only hope for the best. I hope this man TM is as good as you think he is because it's all in his hands."

Morgan was alone when the muffled voice called.

"Is everything set for Thursday?" the muffled voice asked.

"Our man can't make it until Saturday," Morgan said.

"What?" the muffled voice screamed. "You're playing games with me."

"No. No," Morgan said. "He had other commitments and that's the earliest he can make it. I assure you he'll be there on Saturday with the bond."

"He better meet with Ulate at ten a.m. on Saturday. If he doesn't, you'll be very sorry. I know about *Sage,*" the muffled voice screamed and hung up.

Morgan stiffened. His face froze, and his hands started to tremble.

20

When he returned to Boulder, TM briefed Anderson about what he had been asked to do.

"How long will you be gone?" Anderson asked.

"Should be just a few days. I left you a memo that explains where I'll be staying and who I'll be meeting with."

"You sure negotiated a great fee," Anderson said.

"I hope you're right," TM answered.

After checking with his bank and finding that thirty-five thousand dollars had been wired to his account, TM made a one-way reservation on United for his flight from Denver to San Jose. There was a change of planes in Houston, and he was only able to get coach from Denver to Houston, but business class was available for the continuing flight to San Jose. He notified his bank that he would be in Costa Rica and would use his ATM card there as well as the credit card issued by the bank. He also called his cell phone provider and upgraded to international voice, messaging, and data plans.

The flight to Houston was short but not pleasant. He was seated in a middle seat, and there were screaming babies all around him.

During the layover in Houston, he received a text message from Cooper.

Jameson DNA matches killer
thx cc

on way 2 costa rica, he answered.

y, she replied.

business

His flight landed in San Jose on Thursday at eight forty-five in the evening. Even though it was the slow tourist season, there was a long line to go through immigration. As he waited, TM marveled at the immaculate tile floor. The white and light gray tiles were shiny and looked like they had just been buffed. He found an ATM in the baggage area and tried to withdraw colones, but the instructions were in Spanish and he wound up getting US dollars at a premium. His second try was better, and he was able to withdraw two hundred thousand colones, the equivalent of four hundred US dollars.

He rented a car and drove ten miles south on the Pan-American Highway to the Crowne Plaza. When he checked in, he upgraded to a two-bedroom suite so he could have a place for Natalie to stay until they caught a plane. The desk clerk handed him a courier package that he immediately deposited in the hotel safe.

The next morning the hotel concierge marked the location of Rand Trading Company's address on the hotel map of San Jose. It was not within walking distance of the hotel. TM drove the rental car and parked it a block away. He walked past it on the opposite side of the street and saw that it was an elevated one-story building with a faded gray stucco front. The entrance door was set back a few feet and appeared to be behind a metal gate. He looked for the closest place he could park his car and saw a small parking lot a few doors away.

When he returned to the hotel, he considered making plane reservations for Natalie and himself on Sunday but decided to wait until he saw what condition she was in. They would fly to Chicago so she could be reunited with her parents. As Webster had requested, TM texted him that the courier package had arrived.

TM rose early the next morning and retrieved the courier package. He took it to his room and removed the packaging. Inside was a large, sealed manila envelope that he put into a small briefcase. The meeting place was thirty minutes away, but he left the hotel shortly after nine so he would not be late. He parked the car in the small parking lot he had seen and waited until nine forty-five before he left the car. The gate before the building door was locked, but there was a small button on the frame. He pressed the button, and through a small speaker above the door he heard a voice.

"Yes?"

"I'm here to see Mr. Ulate. I have a ten o'clock appointment."

"What's your name?"

"TM," he said.

"TM?" the voice responded.

Before he could respond, he heard a buzzer and was able to turn the gate handle. The door behind the gate was not locked. He opened it and walked up a small staircase to another door. He could see a peephole and was sure he was being watched. He heard what sounded like the sliding of a bolt. He waited a few moments and then opened the door. He stepped into a large room with light-colored wood paneling on the walls and ceiling. At the far end of the room a man was seated behind a large wooden desk. The man was heavyset with deep lines in his face and balding white hair. Although he was seated, he looked to be of short stature. "Mr. Ulate?" TM asked.

"Please sit down," the man said and motioned to a chair in front of the desk. "May I have what you brought?"

"You are Mr. Ulate?" TM asked.

"Of course."

TM reached into his briefcase and handed Ulate the manila envelope. Ulate used a small penknife to open the envelope, being careful not to cut what was inside. He removed an elaborately scrolled brown certificate that bore a wax seal. He then opened a drawer, pulled out a well-worn book, and turned the pages until he found what he was looking for. He opened the drawer again and took out a large magnifying glass that he used to examine the certificate. From time to time he moved the magnifying glass to an image in the book and then back again to the certificate. The process went on for several minutes. When he finished, he pulled a small piece of paper out of the drawer and compared it to the certificate's paper.

"Excuse me for a minute," Ulate said.

He picked up the certificate, got up, and started to walk to a door behind his desk.

"Wait," TM said. "Until I have what I came for, the certificate stays with me."

Ulate dropped the certificate back on the desk and left the room. A few moments later he returned holding a small white envelope in his hands. He handed it to TM. It was sealed.

"Open it," Ulate said. "But don't tell me what's in it. I don't know what this exchange is about, and I don't want to know."

TM tore open the envelope and found an envelope with a key card inside. The envelope bore the name of a hotel and a handwritten room number.

"Is that what you wanted?" Ulate asked.

"I hope so," TM said.

"Let me have your cell phone number," Ulate said.

TM hesitated and then said, "Why do you want it?"

"It's a matter of professional pride. I need to know whether the other side of the bargain has been kept. I will call you tomorrow to find out."

TM wrote the number on a piece of paper and gave it to Ulate.

21

TM had no idea where the hotel was located. The envelope had an address, but it meant nothing to him. He drove back to his hotel and had the concierge locate the other hotel on a map.

"Be careful," the concierge said. "It's not one of the better parts of the city."

TM drove as fast as traffic would allow. When he came to the address of the hotel, he saw a three-story building that was better than he expected. It appeared to be a restored mansion. He drove into the courtyard and parked in a space reserved for new registrants. The room number was 206. TM ignored the elevator and ran up the stairs to the second floor. He found 206 and used the key to open the door. There on the bed in the middle of the room was a woman who was bound and gagged. TM ran to her and undid the gag and bindings.

"Oh thank you," Natalie said, sobbing. "Can you help me escape?"

"Your parents sent me here to get you. You're safe now."

Natalie continued to sob. "I want to go home. I've been so scared. I thought he was going to kill me."

"You're safe now," TM repeated. "Let's get your things and get out of here."

She picked up some clothes from the floor and put them in a large suitcase that was in the corner of the room. She put on her shoes and grabbed a toiletry case from the bathroom. TM extended the handle of the suitcase and pulled it out of the room with Natalie following him.

When they were in the car, TM asked Natalie if she would be able to fly back to the States the next day.

"Yes. Yes. I want to get home and see my parents. It's been such a nightmare. You have no idea how bad it was."

"Were you sexually abused?" TM asked.

"Not sexually but mentally. He was very cruel."

"We'll go to my hotel. I'm sure you'll want to call your parents. They're very anxious to hear from you."

"I can't wait to talk to them," she said.

When they returned to the hotel, TM brought Natalie to the suite and handed her his cell phone.

"You can use this to call your parents. Your bedroom is to the left. I'll let you talk to them alone. When you're finished, you can rest for a while, and then we can have lunch. I'll make plane reservations. But we could have a problem because you probably don't have a passport."

"I do have a passport," she said.

"You better give it to me because I may need it to make reservations," TM said.

All of the flights were full except for flights with two or more stops and long layovers. TM booked a flight on Monday with only one stop and a short layover in Houston.

Several minutes later Natalie came out of the bedroom. "I'm ready for lunch," she said.

While they were in the restaurant waiting for a table, TM asked Natalie how the call went with her parents.

"My mother was beside herself. She could hardly talk she was so excited."

"How about your father?" TM asked.

"He really didn't say very much, and when he did talk, he sounded depressed. Have you met him?"

"No," TM said. "I haven't even talked to him on the phone. All of my dealings were with his lawyer, Daniel Webster."

"Are you a police officer or something like that?" Natalie asked when they were seated.

"No," TM said. "I'm not even a private investigator. I got involved because I have specially trained cadaver dogs and was called in to search an area in the forest next to Flagstaff when you were missing and a body was found."

"Did my parents call the police or the FBI?"

"No. I thought they should and said so several times to Webster. Where were you when you were kidnapped?"

"It's very painful, and I don't want to talk about it," Natalie said. "And certainly not to you."

"So be it," TM said.

Natalie spent the afternoon in her bedroom while TM went on the Internet in the open room. At dinner time he ordered room service after getting her menu selections.

"You've been very quiet," Natalie said while they were having dinner.

"You made it clear that I'm not worth talking to," TM said. "So I'll do my job and get you home to your parents."

"I'm sorry. I didn't mean to offend you. It's just that the ordeal I went through was very painful and I don't like to talk about it."

"OK. It's too bad we couldn't get a flight tomorrow."

22

TM woke early the next morning and went down to the lobby for coffee to bring back to the suite. He was sitting at his computer with the coffee when his cell phone rang.

"Hello," TM said.

"This is Ulate. It's very important that I meet with you."

"I don't understand," TM said. "You said you would call to make sure the bargain was met. It has, so why do we need to meet?"

"Something has come up, and it's urgent that I meet with you."

"Tell me what this is about," TM said.

"No. No," Ulate cried. "I can't explain it on the phone. There is something here at my office that I need to show you."

"This doesn't make sense," TM said.

"Please. Please. I beg you to come."

"All right," TM said. "I'll get there as soon as I can."

TM waited until Natalie came out of her bedroom. "Something's come up and I have to go and meet someone. We'll order breakfast in the room, and then I have to go. When I leave, double-lock the door and don't leave the room no matter what. Do you understand?"

"I don't understand. I thought I was safe."

"You are safe if you follow my instructions. You must lock the main door to the suite and also the door to your bedroom and not open either one until I come back."

TM drove to Ulate's office and parked his car in the same lot as the day before. When he came to the gate at the entrance, he pushed the button, but nothing happened. He tried again without success. He grabbed the handle and to his surprise, was able to open the gate. He walked up the stairs and was able to open the door there as well.

He was stunned by what he saw. An obviously dead Ulate was seated in his chair with his mouth open and a bullet hole in his forehead. In front of him on his desk was the paper with TM's cell phone number. TM stepped closer and took a photo of the body with his cell phone. The door behind Ulate's desk was partially open and TM saw what looked like the bare legs of another body. He carefully pushed the door open and saw a naked man who clearly had been tortured. His genitals had been cut, and there were stab wounds across his stomach and chest. His wide-open eyes and taut face bore an expression of horror. The man had black hair and appeared to be in his late thirties or early forties. TM took several photos, including close-ups of the man's face.

TM drove back to the hotel as fast as he possibly could, frequently passing cars on the wrong side of the road. When he reached the hotel, he parked the car at the front entrance and raced to the suite. He used his card key to enter and shouted Natalie's name. The door to her bedroom opened, and she looked out with alarm.

"What's the matter?" she cried.

"I just saw something horrible," TM said. "And I wanted to make sure you were all right."

"What did you see?"

"I got a call this morning from the man who arranged the ransom exchange. He said he had to see me. When I went there, he was dead. Somebody killed him. I found another body in a room behind the main office. I have photos of him that are very gruesome. I'd like you to look at some of them to see whether you recognize him."

"If they're gruesome, why would you want me to look at them?" Natalie asked.

"Because he might be the kidnapper."

"Why would you think that?"

"When I was there to make the exchange, the intermediary left the room at one point apparently to talk to someone in the other room, the place where I found the body."

"With all I've been through, I'm not up to looking at a gruesome photo now," Natalie said.

"Whether you're up to it or not, this is serious business. Whoever killed those people is still out there. If the other body is that of the kidnapper, the killer has something in mind, and it could mean we're in danger."

He expanded one of the facial photos and handed the phone to Natalie. She screamed and began to sob hysterically.

"Is he the kidnapper?" TM demanded.

"Yes. Yes," Natalie replied, sobbing.

"Do you know his name?"

"No. He never told me."

"You spent several days with this man and he never mentioned his name?"

"No."

"What did you call him?" TM asked.

"I would just say Mister."

"I can't understand why anyone would kill him," TM said. "It might make sense if Ulate double-crossed him, but Ulate is dead too."

"Who is Ulate?"

"He was the intermediary. Whoever killed the two of them undoubtedly took the bearer bond. But the only ones who knew about the bearer bond were your father, Webster, Ulate, the kidnapper, and me. Unless you knew about it. Did you?"

"I don't know what you're talking about. I don't know anything about a bearer bond, and I certainly wasn't in a position to talk to anyone."

"It's all very strange," TM said. "It's a good thing we're leaving tomorrow."

23

The flight to Chicago was scheduled to depart at 11:45 a.m. TM thought it best to be at the airport at least by nine so he could return the rental car and get through the security checkpoints. They checked out of the hotel at eight and loaded their bags into the trunk of the car. As they drove out of the hotel parking lot, a car suddenly pulled in front of them, and two men came out carrying handguns. TM backed up the car, accelerated, and slammed into the rear side of the gunmen's car so it spun around and gave him room to drive away.

Traffic was coming from his left, so he turned right, merged with other cars, and drove as fast as he could to get away from the hotel. He looked in the rearview mirror and saw the gunmen's car in pursuit. He passed several cars and drove at a speed well in excess of the limit. As he drove past an intersection, he saw a San Jose police vehicle and was relieved when he saw that it had turned and was driving after him with its emergency lights flashing and its siren blaring. He drove a little farther and then pulled to the side of the road.

The police car stopped behind him, and two officers got out and started to walk toward his car. The gunmen's car raced by the police officers and screeched to a stop in front of TM's car. The two men got out with their handguns drawn and fired several shots through the windshield at TM and Natalie. But both of them had dropped below the dashboard and were not hit.

The two police officers drew their weapons and began to fire at the gunmen, who returned the fire, hitting one of the officers. TM had not turned off the motor of his car. He sat up, pulled the car to the left, and drove straight into one of the gunmen. The remaining police officer and the remaining gunman exchanged shots, and both of them fell wounded to the ground while TM drove away.

"We can't stay with this car," TM said to a frightened Natalie. "With the holes in the windshield we'll draw too much attention. We'll have to leave most of our luggage behind. Do you have your passport with you?"

"Yes," she said. "But I'll need clothes."

"Clothes are the least of our problems now."

TM noticed a bus terminal ahead on the right and drove the car into the parking lot. He found a space to park the car among several other cars. He grabbed his carry-on from the trunk, and the two of them ran toward the terminal. A line of people was standing at the door of one of the buses.

"Let's get in line," TM said.

"Where is it going?" Natalie asked.

"I have no idea," TM said. "But it'll take us away from here."

As they came to the door, the bus driver asked for their tickets. TM pretended he did not know what was being asked. Finally he pulled out several bills and handed them to the driver. The driver smiled and let them on. Fortunately there were empty seats. As the bus pulled away from the terminal, TM noticed several police cars headed in the direction of the gunfight.

"What about our flight to Chicago?" Natalie asked.

"Forget it. There's no way we can make it. Right now, we want to find a place where we'll be safe until we can figure out a way to get home."

The bus soon reached the outskirts of San Jose. TM could tell that they were on the Pan-American Highway headed north. The highway was three lanes most of the time but occasionally narrowed to two lanes or expanded to four lanes depending on the surroundings. The vegetation on each side of the road was dense except when they passed areas of sugarcane fields, coffee trees, and mangos trees. There were many varieties of trees, including bamboo trees.

The bus stopped every so often and picked up more passengers. It continued on until it reached San Ramon, where there were stores, restaurants, and small hotels. The bus stopped, and several people got off. TM grabbed Natalie's hand, and they got off as well. They walked until TM saw what looked like a hotel that catered to tourists. They approached the check-in counter, and TM told the clerk they wanted a room with two beds.

"I want my own room," Natalie said.

"So do I," TM said. "But I've gone through hell to get you, and there's no way I'm going to let you disappear."

The room was on the second floor and was surprisingly pleasant. It had a balcony that opened onto a courtyard and a small pool. The room was tastefully decorated, and the bathroom had both a bathtub and a shower.

"What am I going to do?" Natalie said. "I don't have any other clothes and no toiletries. Not even a toothbrush."

"Well, you can't borrow mine," TM said. "There's soap in the bathroom. You can wash out your clothes in the sink. I noticed a small shop in the lobby, and when we go down to eat, we'll see what we can find for you. But first I need some answers."

"What do you mean?"

"Things are not what they seem," TM said. "I don't believe you were kidnapped."

"That's outrageous," Natalie snapped. "How can you say that?"

"For several reasons. When I went in the room where you were being held, you didn't look at all like someone who'd been under high stress for several days as a kidnap victim. The bindings on your hands and legs were loose enough that you could have gotten free. And you had this large suitcase. It's passing strange that someone would be kidnapped and be able to bring along a big bag of clothes. But there's more. People don't usually carry around their passports, but you conveniently had yours. Supposedly you were flown to San Jose on a private plane. But your passport was stamped at San Jose International Airport. And when I showed you the face of the dead kidnapper, your reaction was that of someone who knew and liked the kidnapper."

Natalie was stunned. "You're wrong. You're wrong," she said, sobbing hysterically.

"No I'm not. And the sooner you stop lying, the better off we'll be."

"You're cruel," she shouted.

He said nothing but watched as she continued to sob. Finally she stopped and sat quietly.

"It's not as bad as you think," she said softly. "My father is actually my stepfather. He has two kids from his first wife and was always mean to me. He's a very wealthy man, but he never adopted me, and I'm sure I'm not included in his estate plan. I couldn't stand to be at home because of the abuse I took from him. That's why I've been a professional student."

"But what about your mother?" TM said. "You've hurt her worse than anyone can imagine."

"I know, and I feel terrible about that. But I thought it would soon be over and I could make it up to her."

"So who was the supposed kidnapper, and what did you expect to happen?"

"His name is—was—Ken Alexander. I worked at my father's firm during the summers and met Ken one time when I was on a business trip to New York. He was handsome and very smart. We hit it off immediately. He worked for a big investment company and seemed to know all about financial matters. We would visit each other and soon became romantically involved. He'd done some research and found out about gold bearer bonds, which he thought were perfect for ransom because they were difficult to trace since they came from the Middle East."

"Why did he choose San Jose for the exchange?"

"Because he knew Ulate was an expert and could easily tell whether the bond was legitimate. He also knew Ulate could be trusted to act as an intermediary."

"What did you expect to do with the bond?" TM asked.

"Ulate had many contacts. He assured Ken that he could launder the bond and get the proceeds less his commission in an account in Grand Cayman."

"What was his commission?"

"Twenty percent."

"What did you plan to do when the account was opened in Grand Cayman? By the way, in whose name was the Grand Cayman account to be opened?"

"I made sure it was in both of our names."

"So the plan was that someone—it turned out to be me—would rescue you, bring you home to your parents, and everything would be fine and you and Ken would have eight hundred thousand dollars in an account in Grand Cayman."

"That's right."

"Have you told me everything?" TM asked.

"Yes. Yes," Natalie exclaimed.

"But something's missing."

"What do you mean?"

"Nothing you've told me explains why Ken and Ulate were killed and why people are trying to kill us. Did you tell anyone else about your plan?"

"No. Of course not."

"Are you sure you've told me everything?"

"Yes. Yes. I have. My parents will be waiting for me at O'Hare. What do I do?"

"You can use my cell phone. Tell them we missed the flight but will be back as soon as possible. Keep the call short."

24

It was five o'clock, the regular closing time at the law firm where Webster was a partner. He gathered some papers, put them in a briefcase, and headed out of his office. Not too many years before, he would not have left that early but would have continued to work well into the night. But times had changed. Year after year the firm had increased the hourly billing rates so that his hourly billing rate was now $750. Some of the work he did justified such a high rate, but much of the work did not. So many of his clients preferred to work with younger lawyers, even some associates, whose billing rates were much lower. He continued to be the billing partner for these clients but saw the clients' people far less often. He deeply regretted this because he fondly remembered the matters he had worked closely on with officials of clients and had formed close personal relationships with them.

There was one client who was an exception, and that was Jeff Morgan. Morgan and his people made so much money, tons of it, that Webster's billing rate was not an issue. In addition, Morgan seemed more comfortable talking with someone older and more experienced like Webster. Webster also was very knowledgeable about the complex regulations hedge funds were subject to. Thanks to Webster's substantial billings to Morgan's firm, Webster was able to maintain his position in the cutthroat atmosphere that now prevailed in large law firms, including his own.

Webster's office was on LaSalle Street in Chicago, a short walk from the METRA station where he would catch a train to his stop at Central Street in Evanston. He enjoyed the train ride because it gave him time to read the newspaper. He read the *Chicago Tribune* in the morning and the *Wall Street Journal* at night even though by then the financial news was somewhat stale.

When the train reached his station, he stepped off and started to walk toward his home only four blocks away. As he walked, he thought about what the next few years would bring. In a couple of years, he would reach the mandatory retirement age at his firm. His retirement payments would not be as great as the firm used to pay some years before, but he had faithfully contributed money to his profit-sharing account over the years and had managed to make other investments so he and his wife could enjoy a decent standard of living after his retirement.

But it was not to be. As he rounded a corner and was within a few houses from his home, there was a quiet hissing sound of a silencer from a car parked at the curb, and Webster collapsed to the pavement.

25

"I found an ATM nearby," TM said as he and Natalie sat down for breakfast. "I'm limited as to how much money I can take out each day, so I hope we'll find more ATMs in the days ahead."

"Days ahead?" Natalie snorted. "Why don't we just go back to the airport and catch another flight to Chicago?"

"That's not so easy. We're a long way from the airport, and we don't have a car. I was talking to the hotel clerk, and he said if we go to a town about fifty miles from here, there's a small airport that has plane service to San Jose International Airport. He said he could arrange for a driver to take us to the town and the driver will accept US dollars. The driver's price is high, but I have far more dollars than colones."

"Well, let's do that," Natalie said. "Can we leave today?"

"No. The driver's not available until tomorrow. I'm a little concerned about going through the San Jose airport."

"Why is that?"

"I'm sure the San Jose police are looking for me, and they may notify the immigration agents at the airport to be looking for me."

"Why would they be looking for you?" Natalie asked.

"I'm sure they've found the rental car by now, particularly since it has bullet holes in the windshield. They'll trace it back to the rental car company and get my name. It could get very serious. They may think we were involved with the gunmen who shot the policeman. My only hope is to tell them the whole story about the kidnapping and the murders, but it won't help that no law enforcement agency in the United States knows anything about it. The only people they could talk to confirm my story would be Webster and you since I never talked to your father. That doesn't make me feel very comfortable."

"But they probably wouldn't be looking for me. Let me go to the airport and fly home. You can find some way to get back yourself."

"You're a very considerate person," TM said sarcastically. "But you're right. You probably can leave the country without trouble. And it may be easier for me to deal with the situation on my own. Will you tell your parents the true story when you get back?"

"What do you think?" Natalie replied.

"You just answered my question. But don't be so sure the true facts won't come out. By this time, the San Jose police have probably discovered the bodies of Ulate and your friend Ken. And even though Ken was naked, I'm sure there were clothes of his around and even his wallet or other evidence of his identity. They'll see that he was an American and bring in the US consulate or other US government agencies, probably including the Drug Enforcement Agency since the presumption will be that it was drug related. And then they will investigate to find out his background. Somewhere along the way his path and yours will be found to have crossed."

"I doubt they'll connect me to anything, and in any event, it will take them a long time. In the meantime, I can be back in the States."

"OK. We'll let the driver take us to the next town and the airport there tomorrow and get you on a plane to San Jose, where you can catch a flight that connects to another flight to Chicago."

"But," Natalie said hesitantly, "who will pay for the airfare?"

"Guess who? I was given money for expenses, and hopefully there's enough left to pay for your trip. But you better hope they accept my credit card."

"Well, I'm sure there's enough to pay for some decent clothes and toiletries for me to travel. I saw a clothing shop nearby that should have some basic things. My father gave you money to spend on my rescue, and these necessities surely qualify. I've slept in the same room with you and haven't even had a decent nightgown. For all I know, you've been secretly visually exploiting me sexually."

"Those are big words. But don't flatter yourself. My interest in you is anything but sexual. I don't know your father, but I'm beginning to understand why he didn't like you," TM said.

TM went with Natalie to the clothing shop, and the two of them had different thoughts as to what Natalie should buy. She preferred flashy and expensive while he preferred modest and moderately priced.

"The last thing you need now is to be wearing clothes that draw attention to you," TM said.

They finally agreed on relatively bland skirts, pants, and blouses, but TM deferred to Natalie's choice of lingerie and toiletries. They also purchased a medium-sized satchel for Natalie to use for her belongings. TM pulled out his credit card, but the clerk said there would be a surcharge for credit card use. To their surprise, she said her store accepted US dollars and that they were accepted by many stores in Costa Rica.

After a late dinner, they went up to their room and took turns using the bathroom before retiring. When Natalie came out, she was dressed in a short, low-cut nightgown, and the air around her had a fresh scent of perfume. When TM came out of the bathroom, he saw that Natalie was in his bed.

"This may well be our last night together," Natalie said. "So we might as well enjoy it."

"It's very tempting," TM said. "But I don't think your parents would approve if the man they hired to rescue you also fucks you."

"They'd never know," Natalie said.

"Try me again if and when I'm no longer a paid rescuer," TM said and climbed in the other bed.

It was well past midnight when TM was awakened by sounds at the door. Though the room was nearly in total darkness, he was able to make out the form of a man moving toward the bed where Natalie was sleeping. The man turned on a small penlight that dimly illuminated Natalie's body. The light was quickly extinguished, and TM saw the man pull something from his side and lift his arm above his head. With that TM sprang from his bed and grabbed Jameson's ironwood billy stick from the nightstand.

Startled, the man turned to face TM. The first blow of the billy stick smashed the man's arm and forced him to drop the knife he was carrying. The second blow caught him in the temple, and he collapsed unconscious to the floor.

The sound of the blows woke Natalie, and she gasped at what she saw as TM turned on a table lamp. "Oh my God," she shouted. "What happened?"

"We had a visitor, and it's a good thing I didn't accept your invitation last night, because we both would probably be dead."

"Who is he?"

"I have no idea, but there may be more. Stay here and double-lock the door."

"What about him?" Natalie said and pointed at the man on the floor.

"He won't be going anywhere," TM said.

He quickly dressed and left the room with the billy stick. When he reached the lobby, he saw that it was deserted. He stepped out of a side entrance and walked around to the front of the hotel and the parking lot. A car was parked near the entrance with the motor running.

TM stuck to the side of the building, and when he was close to the car, he saw a man behind the steering wheel. He crouched down and crawled to the side of the car just behind the driver's door. He used the billy stick to tap the side of the door. The man turned to see what was making the noise and not seeing anything, opened the door and stepped out.

Seeing TM, the man started to pull a handgun from his belt holster, but before it reached firing level, the billy stick caught him on the bridge of his nose and he dropped to the ground. TM pulled him to the side of the hotel and drove the car to an open spot in the parking lot.

"Grab your things," TM said to Natalie. "We're leaving."

"How?" Natalie asked.

"Just follow me," TM replied.

They placed Natalie's satchel and TM's carry-on in the car and drove away.

"Where are we going?" Natalie asked.

"We're headed to La Fortuna, which is supposed to have an airport," TM said.

"What was that wooden thing you had with you?"

"It was a billy stick."

"What's a billy stick?"

"I'm sure you've seen police officers with clubs hanging on their sides. They're billy clubs, but the billy stick is more lethal. It's longer and made out of a special hard wood. Billy sticks are so lethal that some states only allow them to be carried by police officers."

"But the same states probably say it's all right for anyone to carry a gun."

"We do have a gun. As a matter of fact, two of them. After I disabled the man who had this car, I searched it and found a Glock and a Wilson forty-five, as well as ammunition for both of them."

"Who were these men, and how did they find us?"

"I don't know who they are, but I think I know how they found us."

"How?"

"My cell phone. Apparently whoever they are have access to sophisticated equipment that can track your location by locating the cell towers that pick up your signal. I've turned my cell phone off so hopefully they can't track us anymore. But we've had two close calls from people who have tried to kill us. Actually, they were more interested in killing you."

"Why do you say that?" Natalie asked.

"The bullet holes in the windshield of our car in San Jose were mostly on your side. And the man tonight was looking to kill you. There's a reason why they want you dead, and you know what it is. So we have this situation. The police in San Jose and probably throughout Costa Rica are looking for me. Meanwhile, some people, we don't know who they are, are looking to kill you. So when we get to the airport in the next town we'll find a plane that can take you to San Jose International Airport and I'll find some means of transportation that will get me out of Costa Rica without going through immigration or checkpoints."

"So I'll be on my own?" Natalie cried softly.

"That's right," TM said.

"But I need you. I won't feel safe without you."

"And I'll feel safer without you. If you're not around, I won't be in the middle if men come to kill you."

"But you've been paid to rescue me."

"I did," TM said. "I can't help you anymore unless I know what I'm dealing with. You know more than you've told me."

"You're right. But I'm tired. Let's find a place to get some sleep, and I'll tell you the full story tomorrow."

They drove until they came to Angeles Sur and a small roadside motel. TM woke up the owner, and they were led to a small, one-room facility. There was only one bed, but it didn't matter. Neither of them had any thoughts about making love. But Natalie did fall asleep with her arms around TM.

After they showered and dressed the next morning, they found a café where they had breakfast seated at an outdoor table with a great view of the countryside.

"I don't know where to start," Natalie said. "None of this would have happened if Ken hadn't lost his cool."

"What do you mean?"

"He thought my father was not cooperating because it took so many calls to get things set up. The final straw for Ken was when my father postponed the meeting date. Ken got so upset that he said something he shouldn't have said."

"What was that?" TM asked.

"He said something like, 'I know all about Sage.'"

"How do you know what he said?"

"Because he made the call from our room at the hotel and I could hear his side of the conversation."

"What is Sage?" TM asked.

Natalie took a deep breath. "It's a massive insider trading ring my father is part of."

"How massive?" TM asked.

"It involves dozens of hedge funds and private investors. They have millions and millions of dollars to spend, and they use it to secure leakers in hundreds of companies and investment advisors. They use highly sophisticated Internet software to spread their trades across international boundaries so they're almost impossible to trace. They leave nothing to chance. They have moles inside the government's regulatory agencies but still communicate in ways difficult for the FBI, the SEC, or other agencies to capture. No e-mails. No voice messages, no text messages. Not even telephone calls."

"How do they do this?" TM asked.

"In many ways. For example, they'll have someone post what appear to be innocuous videos on YouTube that actually contain coded messages. They'll have video conferences where people talk about serious financial matters in the news while someone in the background is using sign language to send a coded message."

"How do you know all this?" TM asked.

"From Ken," Natalie replied. "I told you he worked for a big investment company in New York. He got curious when he saw numerous small trades that always seemed to be profitable. He did some snooping and seduced a woman trader who, after a few drinks, let some things slip while he was making love to her. He started to put various pieces together and was able to learn how it worked and who all was involved."

"How do you know your father was involved?" TM asked.

"Ken found out and tipped me off to some things I could do to make sure."

"Is he one of the leaders of the ring?"

"No. When Ken said that he knew about Sage, my father must have panicked and got word to someone who is a leader. They must have decided Ken had to go and sent hit men here to kill him. After what happened last night, it's finally dawned on me that when the hit men tortured Ken, he must have told them that I also know about Sage. That's why they're after me."

"It's hard to believe they would resort to violence and try to have people killed," TM said. "Breaking the insider trading laws is one thing, but murder is another matter."

"There's too much at stake. If what they're doing is exposed, it would not only take down many wealthy people but also their leakers, moles, some government people, and even some members of Congress. I know you didn't think very much of me for trying to get ransom money from my father with the excuse that he had abused me. But I knew that much of his wealth was obtained illegally, and right or wrong, that made it easier for me to take some of it from him. It was wrong of me to do what I did and particularly cruel of me to put my mother through this."

TM sat quietly with a look of disbelief.

"I'm scared," Natalie cried. "What are we going to do?"

26

The couple walking their dog in the park next to Wilmette Harbor barely noticed the two men sitting on a park bench near the lakefront even though they were engaged in an intense conversation. The one with gray hair, blue jeans, and a blue jacket was pleading. But the other man shook his head from side to side with a steely look of rejection. The gray-haired man looked down and began to sob. With that, the black-haired man got up and walked away. After a few minutes, the gray-haired man, with tears streaming down his face, got up and slowly walked to the parking lot, where he stepped into his Mercedes sedan with the initials JTM. They stood for Jeffery T. Morgan.

The other man, Maison Bertre, walked quickly to a waiting limousine that sped away.

When Morgan arrived at his home, he parked the car in the driveway and slowly walked to the front door. With trembling hands, he opened the door and stepped inside. He walked up the stairs, crossed the floor, and opened the door to the spacious master bathroom. He saw the small stepladder first and then the body of his wife, who was dangling from a thin rope tied to the copper ceiling fixture they both had loved. Morgan fell to the floor and cried uncontrollably.

During the viewing at the funeral home and following the funeral, several people asked Morgan why Natalie wasn't there.

"She's in a foreign country," Morgan said, "and couldn't get back in time."

Some thought this was not a very good answer, but no one thought to question Morgan because of his deep grief.

27

The white panel truck parked in front of Ulate's office had no markings. It was used to haul bodies to what some people called the last stop, San Jose's morgue. It was a busy place, and one worker there euphemistically said people should make reservations. There were enough murders that the chief crime investigation unit, the Judicial Investigative Bureau, had strict criteria for determining which murders would be assigned to the top investigators and in what order. OIJ, as it was called, had its own bureaucracy. The agents assigned to investigate the murder of Ulate and Ken were near the bottom of the roster. They did take several photos of the bodies and made sure they had sufficient information so they could fill in many of the blanks of the standard investigation form. The clothes found near Ken's body had his passport, which enabled them to enter his full name and all the other information a passport contains.

One of the boxes to be checked on the form was whether an autopsy should be performed. From experience, they knew to be very cautious about checking the box. There were only so many people qualified to perform autopsies, and their time was not to be wasted. People at their level on the roster were not expected to check the box, so they did not. The bodies of Ulate and Ken were placed in body bags, loaded into the panel truck, and placed alongside the other body bags the drivers had accumulated.

The shooting incident involving the police officers and the gunmen had much higher priority. One of the officers was dead, and the other was seriously wounded. This placed the investigation at the top of the list and drew the attention of OIJ's top investigator, Chief Investigator Roberto Diaz. Under his direction, the crime scene was thoroughly investigated. Photos were taken from every angle, footage was calculated between every possible action point, an autopsy was performed on the deceased officer and gunman, and ballistics tests were performed on all the firearms found at the scene. Both the surviving gunman and the surviving police officer were in critical condition and could not be questioned.

The police car did have a video recording device that showed TM's rental car being pursued and stopped and parts of the ensuing gun battle. It also showed TM's car being driven away. Diaz ordered all police units to look for the car, and it was soon located in the parking lot where TM had left it.

Diaz had initially thought the gunmen were trying to keep the police officers from arresting the occupants of the car. But the bullet holes in the windshield told a different story. The gunmen were trying to kill the people in the car, particularly the passenger. The license plate of TM's car was traced and found to be a rental car with TM identified as the renter. The license plate of the other car was of a stolen vehicle. Neither the deceased gunman nor the surviving gunman had any identification.

Diaz called a meeting of his staff to review what they had found.

"It surely looks like the target car was being pursued by the gunmen and that's why it was speeding and passing other cars," Diaz said. "My first reaction is that both the occupants of the target car and the gunmen's car were drug dealers and this was just another drug war. But we need to look further. The car's renter was identified as a TM. That sounds fishy to begin with because it's just initials. I want you to find out whether there is such a person and if there is, what he's about. Also, let's run the fingerprints of the gunmen and see what we can find."

Alajuella, the district that included San Roman, did not have nearly as many OIJ investigators as San Jose. There also were fewer murders, so the staff did not have such rigid investigative criteria. Investigator Feliz Montero had worked for OIJ in San Jose for several years and had seen everything. More than he had ever wanted, so he had asked for a transfer to the district. Unlike Diaz, Montero only had one assistant. When he arrived at the hotel where TM and Natalie had been staying, he saw the body of a man outside the hotel and was led by a frightened hotel staff member to one of the hotel rooms where he found another. There was no need to check the boxes for an autopsy. Both men had died of severe blunt force trauma to the head. Identification found on the men disclosed they were Costa Ricans.

"The man found in the hotel room must have been an intruder," Montero said to his assistant. "The door to the room appears to have been broken into, and there was a knife on the floor next to one of the beds. The room was registered to a TM, and the clerk who checked him in said he was with a woman. Things don't make sense. The man and the woman didn't call for help, and they've disappeared. The two men got here somehow, and the fact that one of the bodies was at the front of the hotel near the parking lot suggests that they came in a car and the man called TM and the woman must have taken it. TM used a credit card and listed an address in Colorado in the United States. Let's see what we can find out about him."

Sgt. Roger Barrett of the Evanston Police Department was puzzled. Murders in Evanston were infrequent, but they usually fell into one of three categories. Most often a murder was gang related and usually involved narcotics. Less common were domestic violence killings. In rare cases an attempted burglary resulted in murder. But Daniel Webster's death didn't fit any of these. It certainly wasn't a drive-by shooting. It was carefully planned and executed and resembled an organized crime assassination. But as far as Barrett had been able to determine, Webster would not have been a candidate for such a murder. He was a well-known and respected Chicago attorney and had been active in many Evanston charities and cultural organizations.

The murder not only was big news in Evanston; it was highlighted on the front pages of Chicago newspapers and was a lead story on local television news. The Evanston Police Department came under intense public pressure to solve the murder, and the police chief met frequently with Sergeant Barrett and other officers working on the case.

"Obviously someone had a reason to kill him," Barrett said to the Evanston Police Chief. "We have to find the reason. I have men interviewing his family, business associates, and friends. We're also trying to get his bank and other financial records and are looking at his computer hard drives for anything that might give us a clue. We're also getting his telephone records, not only at home and at the office but also his cell phone records. Fortunately the family is cooperating fully."

28

The most secure room in the United States is the White House Situation Room in Washington, DC. Every possible precaution has been taken so that nothing that takes place there can be intercepted by anyone. The second most secure place is a room in the lower level of an old brownstone mansion on Park Avenue in New York City.

"I don't understand why the people you hired were not able to eliminate Morgan's daughter," Bertre said in the secure room to Alfred Cragin.

Bertre, who was in his mid-fifties, had a dark complexion and black hair. He wore a black suit with an open-collared black shirt that disguised somewhat that he was overweight.

Cragin was in his late forties and was built like a football running back, which at one time he was. He wore his brown hair short, almost in a crew cut.

"The man Morgan hired to bring his daughter home has been protecting her," Cragin said.

"Who is he?" Bertre asked.

"His name, believe it or not, is TM, and he's tough and very resourceful. Our people got his cell phone number and have been tracking his location. They last located him at a small hotel several miles outside San Jose, but the men we sent to get him and the daughter have been unreachable. We think they're either dead or in jail."

"Can they be traced back to us?"

"Absolutely not. We go through various people to hire our killers, and they don't know anything other than what they're paid to do. Unfortunately, we aren't able to track him anymore. He must have figured out what we were doing and ditched his cell phone."

"We have to find him," Bertre exclaimed.

"We will. Morgan wired funds to TM's bank account and gave us the number. We, of course, can access account information and have someone watching the activity online. TM has been using ATMs to withdraw money and likely will have to continue doing that, and we can track the ATM's location."

"But that only tells us what town he's in and not where he is in the town," Bertre said.

"But there are only so many towns in Costa Rica, and we have more people looking for them," Cragin said.

"What if they go back to the San Jose airport?"

"We have all the airport entrances covered. There's no way our men will let them get by."

"But what if they drive by car or bus on the Pan-American Highway to the United States?" Bertre asked.

"We've got them listed in the highest category of terrorist suspects, and the immigration authorities and border patrols have been given a red alert to be on the lookout for them. If they cross the border, they will immediately be taken into custody. Instructions have been given that they are not to be questioned or allowed to talk to anyone. The authorities have been given a number to call to reach a top secret antiterrorism unit that will come and get TM and the woman. They'll be put on a plane and flown to a foreign country, where they'll be turned over to that country's intelligence people, who will make them disappear. I wondered if we should do something about Morgan."

"No. There's too much going on around him," Bertre said. "I think you were successful in having his wife's death look like a suicide. But with her death and the death of Morgan's lawyer, Morgan's death would raise all kinds of red flags. I don't think he'll do anything stupid."

"OK. But we'd better keep our eye on him."

29

As TM drove from Angeles Sur to La Fortuna, he came into what the local people called the Cloud Forest. They gained altitude as they drove and at times were forced to pull over to the side of the road because of dense fog. The road was very curvy, and at times they came to bridges that only one vehicle could go over. On either side of the road was dense vegetation. They finally came to a stretch of the road that had fewer curves, with local cattle and horses on either side as well as fields of sugarcane, rice, and plantain. The cattle were Brahmans, and most of the horses were paints.

As they drove into La Fortuna, TM and Natalie were greeted by a spectacular view of Arenal, one of Costa Rica's active volcanoes. The streets were full of tourists visiting the small shops that sold souvenirs and other attractions.

"We'll stay here overnight and try to figure out what to do next," TM said.

"Should we try to fly to San Jose and get a flight to somewhere in the States?" Natalie asked.

"We've already talked about that," TM said. "It's far too risky. We'll have to figure something else out."

TM was able to book a large room with two beds at Hotel Fortuna. The room had a good view of Arenal volcano from a private balcony, but they were not there for the scenery. The top of the volcano was covered with clouds and rain began to fall, which was not unusual because they were there at the beginning of the rainy season. After they had settled in, they sat down in the room's small seating area.

"We don't have many options," TM said. "We need to get out of Costa Rica and to another country where it's unlikely the authorities or the men who are after you would be looking for us. Hopefully we can then catch a flight to the States."

"How do we get to one of those countries?" Natalie asked.

"Plane, car, bus, or boat," TM said.

"How could we get a plane if we can't go to San Jose?"

"We might be able to hire someone with a small plane. Unfortunately, that would cost a lot of money, and that's something we don't have. That leaves car, bus, or boat. We have a car, but we can't be sure the police or the bad guys won't be looking for it. It probably would be better to go by bus. People travel a lot by bus here, so that might be a good option if we can find bus routes that go to the right places. It might also be easier for us to cross the border if we're on a bus. We're a long way from Panama, so it might be better to go to Nicaragua."

"What about a boat?" Natalie asked.

"A boat could be terrific for getting us out of Costa Rica and into another country without having to go through border checkpoints," TM said. "But finding the right place where we can get our own boat or someone to take us in theirs is a problem."

"So what do we do now?"

"The hotel has Wi-Fi, so I can try to find information about bus routes and schedules. If we're lucky, I might also find ways to get to the ocean and charter a boat. But we need more money. I'll e-mail my assistant, Jim Anderson, and ask him to wire me some funds. But first, I need to get a new cell phone so I can call him and give him some idea about our problems and why I need the money. We probably should get backpacks because there's no telling how we're going to be moving around and it may not be so easy to carry bags."

"Can I go with you?" Natalie asked.

"It's probably best you don't," TM said. "We can't rule out the possibility that the bad guys are in the area looking for us, and if they are, we're much easier to spot if we're together."

"I just had an idea."

"What?"

"We should change our identities."

"Good idea. How do we do that?"

"I can dye my hair and you can grow a beard."

"The hair dying part makes sense, but it takes time to grow a beard."

"You can shave your head. That's even fashionable now."

"No thank you. I like my hair. I'll let it grow as I grow a beard, and in the meantime I'll wear a skullcap. I thought you already dyed your hair blond. Can you let it go to your natural color?"

"That'll take longer than you growing a beard," Natalie said. "I wonder where I can get the stuff to color my hair."

"We're kidding ourselves," TM said. "I doubt any killers would know our features very well. They'll be looking for a man and a woman in their early thirties to forties who are not Hispanic and don't look or act like tourists. So it's OK for us to change our hair and me to grow a beard, but that may not be enough if they're after us."

"So when we're out in public we need to hold hands and act like lovers," Natalie said.

"A little bit of that is all right, but let's not get carried away," TM said.

31

Jim Anderson had programmed different ring tones on his cell phone. The one for his wife was a harp. For TM it was a bugle. But now, as he was training a new dog to become a drug sniffer, he heard just the default ring tone. He looked down at his phone and didn't recognize the number. In fact, it was a number from a different country, so he ignored it. When he had finished the training session, he noticed he had a voice mail. He walked back to his office and after checking his e-mails, listened to the message.

"Jim," the voice said, "it's TM. Big problems here. You can't call me so I'll try to call you again in a few minutes."

Anderson cancelled his plans for fieldwork with the dogs and went to the best place for cell phone reception just outside the front door to the building.

He waited for what seemed like an eternity before his phone rang again. He saw it was the same foreign number from before.

"Hi, TM," he said. "What's happening?"

"I was able to get the girl, but all hell has broken loose," TM said. "For reasons I can't tell you over the phone, people are trying to kill her, and now they're after me as well. We need to get out of Costa Rica, but we can't go by plane. I really need money. I located a bank in La Fortuna that will accept a wire transfer for up to five thousand US dollars and give me the equivalent in Costa Rican currency. I'll e-mail you the wiring instructions. I can't use my regular cell phone because the killers were using it to track me. I bought a cell phone here and will try to call you from time to time."

"Should I contact the State Department or law enforcement here?" Anderson asked.

"No," TM said. "Even that may not be safe."

"This is incredible," Anderson said.

"More incredible than you could ever imagine."

32

TM had to walk a few blocks to get to the bank. The sidewalks were uneven, and in several places the concrete had broken into pieces. The most beautiful structure by far was the Catholic church. It was painted a tan color and was located across from a small park. The bank was crowded when TM went in to get the wired funds. It had a small lobby and only three tellers. He had waited several hours to give the transfer time to be completed and wasn't sure if the money had arrived.

When he finally reached the front of the line, the teller did not understand English, so there was a delay while she went to find a bank employee who did. A heavyset woman who looked like a supervisor came to the window and agitatedly asked TM what he wanted. When he told her, she asked him to step aside and let others be served while she checked to find out whether the funds were there. After several minutes she reappeared and motioned for TM to go to a desk at the side of the room.

"I need proper identification," the woman said officiously.

"Here is my passport," TM said.

She opened the passport and leafed through the pages before coming back to the front to his photo. She looked at it closely and then looked at him.

"This doesn't look like you," she said. "Do you have any other identification?"

TM pulled out his wallet and handed the woman a credit card and his ATM card.

"How do I know you didn't steal these?" she said.

"I don't know what you're trying to do, but it's quite clear that I'm the person for whom the wire was intended," TM said. "It can't be a coincidence that money would arrive from the United States for someone with my name and that an imposter would suddenly appear to collect the funds. And if you look again at the passport photo you'll see that it's my photo. So let's stop the nonsense and get me the money. If it will help matters, I'll give you one hundred thousand colones for your troubles."

"That's insulting," the woman said and got up and walked to a back office.

A few moments later she reappeared with a large envelope and pulled out several stacks of bills.

"Each band lists the amount of bills it contains," the woman said. "You can count the numbers on the bands, but I don't have time for you to count each bill separately. The total reflects the five percent fee the bank charges."

"I'll take your word for that," TM said. "What about the amount I promised you?"

"I don't accept bribes," the woman said. "You have what you came for, so just leave."

TM took the envelope and placed it in his backpack. He left the bank and walked toward the hotel a few blocks away. He had only gone about a block when he had the feeling he was being followed. He glanced over his shoulder and caught a glimpse of two men on the other side of the road looking at him intently. He decided to walk where there were crowds of people so it would be less likely the men would attack him and he would also have the opportunity to elude them. He came to a large square with many different booths and many people. Instead of walking straight, he darted between the booths and turned back in the opposite direction until he came to a building with a large arcade and shops on either side. He ducked into a large shop that featured T-shirts, pottery, and other tourist items and went to the corner of the store where he could see people passing by in the arcade.

After several minutes he went to the entrance of the shop and, after seeing no one unusual in either direction, walked into the arcade and headed back to the square. Rather than walk directly back to his hotel, he decided to take a lengthier route that would be more crowded with people. He had walked less than a block when he was startled to see Natalie walking in his direction. When she spotted him, she ran toward him. It was the last thing he wanted, because it made it much easier for any men sent by the insider trading ring to identify the two of them.

His concern was well placed because no sooner had Natalie reached him than two men came running up from behind him. As the men got closer, they raised their handguns and prepared to fire. But they were not the only men after TM.

The bank supervisor had a plan of her own. Her initial delay in meeting with TM was to give her time to call her husband and alert him that an American would be leaving the bank with several thousand colones in cash. The husband called his friend, and the two of them were waiting when TM left the bank. They were careful to blend in with other people on the street and waited for the right opportunity to accost TM and take the money. When they saw the other two men about to act first, the husband and his friend jumped the two men and wrestled with them for control of the handguns. One of the men fired his handgun, but his arm was jolted and the shot went into the air. The gunshot created panic in the streets as some women screamed and people ran in different directions.

TM grabbed Natalie's hand, and they ran with a group of people until they were able to make their way back to their hotel.

"We have to leave immediately," TM said. "Pack everything you can into your backpack as fast as you can."

"Where will we go?" Natalie cried.

"We'll drive the car to a place where we'll abandon it and walk to a small complex of wooden buildings I located earlier. There's a man there who'll take us in overnight and then lead us from here."

"Do you mean walk?" Natalie cried.

"Yes," TM said. "But on horseback."

"That's ridiculous," Natalie said. "I've never been on a horse."

"Well, you have three choices. You can stay here, walk while I ride, or get on a horse. Horseback riding is easy, and you'll quickly learn all you need to know for what we'll be doing."

"But where will the horses take us?"

"I'm told there's a trail that leads around the volcano to a town where we can get a bus. Our guide will have a packhorse with supplies for us to spend one night on the trail. It won't be luxurious, but it will get us away from the killers."

"How did they find us?" Natalie asked.

"Good question," TM said. "Before they were tracking my cell phone, but now I think they have access to my bank account and are tracking where I use an ATM or do any banking. Thank goodness I was able to get the cash Anderson wired even though that created its own problem but may have saved our lives."

"What do you mean?"

"It was no coincidence other men showed up. I'm sure now that the woman at the bank took her time so she could get someone to steal the money. They did us a big favor."

"We can use a lot more favors. I have no idea where we're going or whether I'll ever get back home," Natalie said, sighing.

33

Sergeant Barrett sat uncomfortably in a wooden seat across from the desk of Evanston's police chief. The seat was not intended to make a person comfortable.

"I have to meet with the mayor and some of the city council members late this afternoon, and I'm sure they'll be asking about the Webster murder," the chief said. "What can you tell me that will make them feel good?"

"Not much, I'm afraid," Barrett said. "If he had any enemies, we haven't found them. We've talked extensively to the people at his law firm, and no one there could think of any matter he was working on that would lead someone to kill him. Lawyers' negotiations can get pretty heated but not to the point where there would be a homicide. His family has been very cooperative and gave us access to his banking and brokerage records. We couldn't find any unusual transactions either, with large, unexplained sums going in or coming out. We had some difficulty checking his computers because his firm is concerned about client confidentiality. They had one of their litigators check the computers, and he said he couldn't find anything unusual. We could go to court to get our own access, but I'd rather not do that at this time."

"So you have no leads?" the chief asked.

"I didn't say that. We found some text messages on his cell phone that certainly raised our eyebrows."

"How so?"

"He had some messages that indicated he was frantically trying to get hold of a person."

"Do you know who the person is?" the chief asked.

"It's weird," Barrett said. "Webster's contact listing only has the person's initials, TM. We called the number, but there was no answer. There was a text message to Webster from this TM saying he had the girl."

"What girl?"

"We have no idea. Webster's wife said she doesn't know anything about it either."

"Can't you get the person's address from the phone company?"

"Yes. But not easily. To protect itself, the phone company requires a court order, and we're in the process of getting one."

"How soon before the murder were the text messages sent?" the chief asked.

"Just a few days," Barrett said.

"You may be on to something, but I don't think I'll mention the details in my meeting this afternoon. Anything I say will be leaked to the press within minutes. I'll say we haven't finished interviewing people and hope to have something soon. They'll give me hell for not having solved the case yet, but that goes with my job. Let me know just as soon as you learn more about this TM person."

"Of course," Barrett replied.

Chief Investigator Diaz was not a patient man. He called his two top assistants into a small conference room at OIJ headquarters in San Jose and got right to the point.

"What have you found out about the two gunmen who fired on the police officers?" he demanded.

"The surviving gunman is still in critical condition, and we were not able to question him," Assistant Chief Investigator Hector Munoz said. "But we were able to identify him from his fingerprints. His name is Alfredo Renzi and he has a reputation as a high-priced enforcer. We've heard a lot about his handiwork but have never been able to make a case against him, partly because potential witnesses refuse to talk or they disappear. We think he was hired to assassinate the man known as TM or the woman who was with him, but we don't know who hired him."

"Then get back to work and find out," Diaz barked. "What about the gunman who died?"

"We ran his fingerprints and found he'd been arrested a number of times for mainly petty offenses, but most recently he'd been a Renzi lieutenant."

"What more do you know about this TM person?" Diaz asked.

"The car rental agreement has an address in Colorado," Investigator Rio Rieal replied. "We checked on the Internet and were able to locate a firm called TM Canine and Protective Services. They train dogs for search and rescue, drug detection, and cadaver recovery. They also provide what are in effect bodyguards for rich people."

"Did you call the firm and try to talk to this TM?" Diaz demanded.

"No."

"Why not?" Diaz asked.

"I wanted to get your approval first."

"This doesn't make any sense," Diaz said. "If this TM person is involved with dog training and bodyguard services, why would the gunmen be after him? Weren't the bullet holes on the windshield of the rental car mainly on the passenger side?"

"That's right," Munoz said.

"So the gunmen may not have been after TM at all," Diaz said. "Do we have any idea who the passenger was?"

"No," Munoz said. "But we were able to determine from the video recording in our patrol car that it was a woman."

"Could you tell the color of her hair or any features?"

"Only that she had blondish hair."

"Great," Diaz said. "That narrows it down to hundreds of millions of women. Did the rental car people see the woman?"

"No, only the man. The rental car agent said he had a Colorado driver's license, was about six feet tall, and was fairly trim."

"Was there a picture of him on his company website?" Diaz asked.

"No."

"Call the number of his firm in Colorado and try to speak to him. If you do, tell him who you are and that we are concerned about what might have happened to him. If he is responsive, try to get him to identify the woman and explain why men were after them. If he doesn't answer but someone else does, find out if that person knows where he is and how we can contact him. In the meantime, let's find out who hired Renzi. We must know people who can help us locate that person. We have a dead officer and another seriously wounded. Let's pull out all the stops on this one. If you have to apply extra pressure, do so. But get me the man who hired Renzi."

"What did you find out about the man called TM?" Feliz Montero asked his assistant.

"He gave his phone number when he registered at the hotel. I called and talked to someone but couldn't find anything out. But then I got lucky and found out he's on the United States terrorist list," the assistant replied.

"How did you find that out?" a startled Montero asked.

"I had some training in the United States and got to know a few people there in their Department of Homeland Security. I called one of them and it took a few hours for him to get back to me. When he called back, he first wanted to know why I was asking. When I told him what happened at the hotel, he said that this TM is on their very highest list of terrorists. He said they probably would send agents here to try to locate him."

"I wish you hadn't called him," Montero said.

"Why is that?" the assistant asked.

"Because it only means more hassle for us. They'll send some guys who'll act important and treat us as dummies. What do we know about the two men who were killed? Did they have any identification?"

"Yes. But I haven't had time to check them out."

"Where are they from?"

"San Jose. I'll give the information we have to the OIJ people there and ask them to find out about them."

"Well, you better tell them it's important or they won't get around to it for weeks."

"You better ask them," the assistant said, "because they won't pay much attention to me."

"I will. Where are the bodies?"

"We sent them to the undertaker."

"You better make sure they haven't been disposed of."

34

Carson Cooper couldn't get TM out of her mind. She had had close relationships with three different men in the past, including one who asked her to marry him. Her mother thought he was perfect for her. He had a good job with an insurance company, came from a good family, and was pleasant to be with. They also had a decent sex life. But he scared her when he kept talking about starting a family. He said he expected to move up at his company and she would be able to quit her job and stay home to take care of their children. But that's not what she wanted to do, so she declined his proposal and he broke up with her. She had no regrets, but there were times when she felt very lonely and wondered whether she would ever find someone with whom she could have a close relationship.

Part of her said she should forget TM. He probably was about fifteen years older than her, and maybe she was thinking about him so much because they had had such a dramatic experience. They also had had the best sex of her life. Whatever the reason, she wanted to see him again. She often regretted the fact that she had just left a note instead of leaving after he was awake. *He probably doesn't think much of me after that,* she said to herself, *even though the note was very warm.*

She decided to reach out by sending him a text message. He had texted her and said he was going to Costa Rica on business.

R u back from CR? How was ur trip?

She hoped he would quickly respond, but he did not.

35

The horses were about the same size as TM's Paso Finos. They had a rope bridle and no bit and only a single rope rein. He knew they had had many riders and were not likely to respond to his riding habits such as neck reining.

Natalie warily eyed the horses. Fortunately the clothes she had been able to bring with her included a pair of slacks. But she only had her walking shoes and not a pair of boots. The guide gave her a helmet and told her to wear it, but she refused.

"Don't blame me if you fall off and crack your head," the guide said.

He brought her a twelve-year-old bay gelding and helped her climb into the saddle.

"What do I do now?" she said.

"Take hold of the rein," the guide said, "but don't pull on it. The horse's name is Ace, and he knows what to do. You just stand there until we get started, and Ace will follow my packhorse."

TM walked up beside her on a gray five-year-old mare with a black mane and tail. "When the trail is wide enough, I'll ride beside you," he said. "When it narrows, I'll ride behind you."

"What if I have to relieve myself?" Natalie asked.

"We'll stop, and you can hide behind a bush while you do your thing. But be careful because there are very poisonous snakes to watch out for."

"I've changed my mind," Natalie said. "I'll go back and take my chances. It'll probably be a lot safer than doing this."

"Very well," TM said and climbed off his horse.

"I'll help you get off and you can be on your way."

"But aren't you coming with me?" Natalie cried.

"No, but I can't stop you if you're so foolish as to go back to the town. I have no idea where you'll stay or what you'll do once you get back. But that's your problem."

"I've changed my mind," Natalie said. "But promise me you'll watch out for snakes."

"I'll do the best I can, but be careful where you walk," TM said.

"Are there lions or tigers or anything like that?" Natalie asked.

"No lions or tigers. There are some jaguars around here, but we'll never be lucky enough to see one."

"Lucky?" Natalie cried.

"Yes. Lucky. They're very beautiful animals, but they stay away from people."

The guide started riding, and TM and Natalie followed. They soon found they were not alone on the trail. During the first part of the ride they encountered other riders coming in the opposite direction and occasionally were passed by other riders whose horses were trotting rather than walking. Two riders passed them at a canter, which scared Natalie but not her horse.

They rode in silence until Natalie suddenly exclaimed, "I've made a mess of my life."

"What do you mean?" a startled TM said.

"I should have settled down and gotten a job rather than keep going to school. If I'd done that we wouldn't be in this situation now."

"Why didn't you?"

"I wasn't happy when my mother remarried, and I started acting out."

"What happened to your father?" TM asked.

"He killed himself."

"Why?"

"He thought he was a failure. My mother was this beautiful, vibrant person with many friends, and he started to think he wasn't good enough for her. He worked as an accountant with a small manufacturing company and had no hope of advancing. He saw his wife's friends with beautiful clothes and a county club life and he couldn't afford to have the same for her."

"Did she resent that?" TM asked.

"She never said so, but there were times you could see she was hurting when her friends were doing things she couldn't do."

"How old were you when he died?"

"Fifteen. I'll never forget it because I'm the one who found his body. I came home one day and he was sitting in his car in the garage with the door down and the motor running. He had attached a hose to the exhaust and had the other end through a window in the car with the other windows closed. I pressed a button to open the garage door and tried to open the car door, but it was locked. So I called nine-one-one. There was nothing they could do."

"How did you get along with your father?" TM asked.

"I adored him, but I also felt sorry for him because I could see he was miserable. He was very good to me. It didn't take long after his death for my mother's friends to fix her up with my stepfather. He had recently divorced his wife and was considered a good catch. They married when I was seventeen. He's been good to my mother and gotten her the things she never had, so she now goes to the country club with her friends.

"I resented him, and it didn't help that he preferred his children from his first marriage. My acting out led to fights with my stepfather that made my mother feel bad, so I escaped by going to school. My dislike of him turned to disgust and even hatred when I found out he was involved with the insider trading scheme. I thought of my father, who was a kind, decent man who thought he was a failure because he could only have a financially modest life for his family while my stepfather was living the high life with fancy cars and many social events mainly as the result of cheating."

"I understand you better now," TM said. "We'll find a way to get out of this mess, and then you can make a new start."

Natalie turned to him. "Do you really think so?"

"Yes," TM said firmly.

36

The National Counterterrorism Center was quick to send word to Norm Rogers, its sole agent in Costa Rica, that TM, a high-level terrorist suspect, was in Costa Rica and should be apprehended. He was advised that additional agents were being dispatched to assist him in the effort.

Rogers was on assignment to NCTC from the CIA and used San Jose as a base for his operations in Central America. He was in his early fifties, and there were signs of gray in his dark hair. He kept himself trim by running six miles virtually every morning. Even though he was not Hispanic, his dark features allowed him to blend in with the local people, and he was fluent in Spanish.

The communication he received had few details about the man he was supposed to find. It said he had murdered two men in the small town of Angeles Sur. He was told to drive there and meet with the local OIJ people, who would provide him with more details.

Bertre was livid.

"How could your people screw up again?" he screamed at Cragin. "This is the third time they let him get away. What kind of idiots are they?"

"We've had incredibly bad luck," Cragin responded. "Plus this guy TM is very difficult to deal with. But we're getting help from the government."

"What!" Bertre screamed as his face grew red.

"Yes. The police in a town where he killed two of our people found out that TM is on the terrorist list and contacted Homeland Security. They immediately got in touch with NCTC, and they're assigning agents to get TM."

"No! No! No!" Bertre shouted. "We have to stop that."

"Why?" Cragin demanded.

"Because it's out of the country, the CIA is involved, and they're going to want to know a lot more than we want anyone to know. We have set it up so that when TM and the girl try to enter the country, a special domestic unit will get involved and do rendition."

"How do we stop the CIA?" Cragin asked.

"It's going to be very difficult and very touchy. We're going to have to go to people high up in government who are taking money from us. But it's very delicate because they don't want to get directly involved. They usually work through underlings. If they'll do it, it's going to cost us a small fortune. What else are you doing to find them?"

"We sent down a new team, and these people are probably the best there is."

"What are they going to do?" Bertre asked.

"They're going to the last place we know TM and the girl were. These guys were contract security people in Iraq until they got caught running their own contract killing operation that cost the lives of some people our government considered strong allies. They'll scour the area until they locate them."

"What do these new men know about our operation?" Bertre asked.

"Nothing. They've been told that TM and the girl defrauded a very wealthy man out of millions of dollars and there's a big reward if they find them and bring them back dead or alive. They've also been told that TM is a dangerous killer and they may have to kill him first. We also told them they need not spare the girl."

"For your sake, this better work," Bertre quietly said.

37

Anderson answered the first call he received from Costa Rica because he thought it might be TM. Instead, it was from a police official in Costa Rica wanting to know about TM and where he could be found. Anderson asked the caller why he was calling but did not receive a satisfactory response. The call was followed by others from Costa Rica, but Anderson soon stopped answering the phone and let the calls go to his voice mail.

Periodically Anderson would listen to his voice messages. The callers from Costa Rica left phone numbers, but he did not return any of the calls. One of the voice mails was from Carson Cooper.

"Hi, Jim, this is Carson Cooper. I'm sure you'll remember me from Flagstaff. TM told me he was going to Costa Rica on business. I've been trying to reach him, but he doesn't respond to text messages and doesn't answer his phone. I just want to make sure he's OK. You can reach me at 303-899-2211."

Ever since the call from TM, Anderson had struggled with what he should do. TM had told him not to contact any law enforcement person because what was happening was "more incredible than you could ever imagine."

I need to talk to someone, Anderson thought, *because I just can't do nothing.* Carson was a law enforcement person, but she was different. She and TM had shared a life-threatening experience, and although Anderson did not know the extent of their relationship, he knew they were more than friends. He decided to take a chance. He called her from his office phone.

"Hello," she answered.

"Carson, this is Anderson. TM is in trouble, and I'd like your help in figuring out what to do."

"What happened?" she cried.

"I don't want to talk it about on the phone. Can I meet you somewhere? I can pay for you to fly here or I can go where you are."

"I can take tomorrow, Friday, off. If I fly in to Stapleton early tomorrow, can you meet me at the airport?

"Of course. E-mail me your flight information and I'll be there to meet you. I'll e-mail you my cell phone number and you can call me when you arrive."

Cooper booked an early morning flight from Sky Harbor to Denver with an early evening return flight the same day. She e-mailed Anderson her flight number and arrival time. Because of the late booking, the round trip airfare was substantial, even though she had to settle for a middle seat in economy.

The fact that she was a law enforcement officer gave her no priority in going through security, but fortunately the line was not long. After displaying her boarding pass and driver's license, she put her briefcase with an iPad and a small plastic bag with her cosmetics on the belt for the x-ray machine.

As much as she recognized the need for airport passenger security, she hated the process. Her law enforcement training emphasized the need to be polite to people even when they were under investigation. Many of the TSA personnel acted as though there was a presumption that all passengers were terrorists. They barked orders and frequently displayed a lack of common sense. This happened with Cooper. She went into the full-body scanner and was asked to step aside for further examination. The machine had detected two metal items on her body-a chain bracelet and an antique coin hanging from a thin rubber necklace.

A female TSA person was summoned who turned the bracelet around as if it were somehow concealing some kind of weapon, something that only a TSA person could consider even remotely possible. The necklace was considered so potentially dangerous that Cooper was asked to remove it so it could be run through the x-ray machine.

When she boarded the plane, her bad luck continued. Seated next to her in the window seat was a lady holding a one-year-old who was not at all happy with the experience. The aisle seat was amply occupied by a man who weighed at least 350 pounds, many of which folded over the armrest into what was supposed to be her space. He promptly unwrapped a breakfast burger that overflowed with mayonnaise and chunks of tomato. Fortunately the flight left on time and arrived on time.

Shortly after Carson's call, Anderson pulled up in a Ford F150 pickup to the front of the terminal where Cooper was waiting.

"How was your flight?" Anderson asked.

"You don't want to know." Cooper sighed. "Tell me about TM."

"I'd rather wait until we get to our office."

"How long will that take?"

"About an hour."

"How long have you been working with TM?"

"About five years."

"He told me he was in Afghanistan."

"He went there as a lieutenant in the Rangers shortly after nine/eleven. He was with a group of Special Forces who were ambushed by a large contingent of Taliban fighters. It almost ended in total disaster. TM was with four or five other soldiers on a mountain ridge. The Taliban fired at them from higher positions, and there was very little cover. TM's group was pinned down but managed to return fire and kill several Taliban. But a Taliban fighter fired a rocket that killed some of the soldiers with TM, and he was seriously wounded. He was lucky to survive. Just as the Taliban were about to overrun his position, a relief group came and rescued him. He was flown back to the States, where he wasn't expected to survive. But he did. It took him months to recover. The only sign of his injuries is a slight limp."

"I noticed that," Cooper said. "How did he get into the dog-training business?"

"It came later. He was hired by the Drug Enforcement Agency to go back to Afghanistan and work with them to find drug dealers. But he was too successful, and the State Department had him sent back to the States because he was closing in on people close to the top Afghans. When he got back, he recruited some of his former army buddies and started a personal protection service. It's been very successful. His people provide personal protection for business executives, sports figures, and celebrity entertainers. While he was in Afghanistan he saw a canine team from Australia do amazing mine detection and other work with dogs and decided to expand into dog training. I was working with dogs, and he hired me to help him. I also manage the personal protection business."

"Does he have a family?" Carson asked.

"No. He was married a few years ago, but his wife was killed by a hit man for a drug lord."

"How awful."

"He was devastated."

They rode in silence until they reached TM's office. Anderson gave Cooper a brief tour of the facilities and then took her to a small conference room where his secretary had set out coffee and soft drinks.

"TM and I were in Flagstaff because we were hired by a wealthy investor to look for his missing daughter who was a student at NAU. After a body was found in the Coconino forest, we conducted a search to rule out the possibility that the daughter also had been murdered and buried.

"While we were in Flagstaff, TM got a call that the daughter had been kidnapped and was being held for ransom. The kidnapper was in San Jose, Costa Rica, and demanded that he receive a million-dollar gold certificate. Against the strong advice of TM and the investor's lawyer, the investor didn't contact the FBI. For whatever reason, neither the investor nor his lawyer was up to going to Costa Rica. They were desperate and prevailed upon TM to go there and make the exchange. But a couple of days went by and he wasn't back. Then TM called from a cell phone other than his own and left me a voice mail. He said there was a big problem and he would call me again. A little while later he called again, and this time I answered. I've been reliving his words ever since."

"What did he say?" Cooper asked with a pained expression on her face.

"He said he'd been able to get the girl but all hell had broken loose. People were trying to kill them. He said, and these are his words, 'There have been some bad incidents, and they think I'm a criminal.' He said he needed money and asked me to wire five thousand dollars to a bank in La Fortuna, Costa Rica, which I did. I asked him whether I should contact the State Department or law enforcement here, but he said that wouldn't be safe. I said this was incredible, and his last words were, 'More incredible than you could ever imagine.' I haven't heard from him since."

"I'm stunned," Cooper said.

"Now you know why I didn't want to get into this on the phone or even during our ride from the airport. I've been agonizing about what I should do, and when you called, I decided I had to share this with someone, and I know TM trusts you. Maybe the two of us can think of something. Lately I've even been getting some calls from a police official in Costa Rica asking about TM."

"What did you tell him?"

"I didn't say anything during the first call and haven't answered the others. They went to my voice mail."

The phone in the conference room rang, and Anderson answered. He turned to Cooper and said, "It's our secretary. There's a man on the line who says he's a policeman in Evanston, Illinois, and wants to talk to TM. I'll tell her to say he's not here."

"No," Cooper said. "Tell her to put the call through to here. Is there a speakerphone?

"Yes." Jim pushed a button on the phone. "This is Jim Anderson, TM's assistant. I have you on the speakerphone with Carson Cooper. Who's calling?"

"Sergeant Barrett of the Evanston Police Department. I'd like to talk to someone called TM."

"Why are you calling?" Cooper asked.

"I'd like to talk to this TM," Barrett replied. "Is he there?"

"No," Anderson said. "He's away."

"Do you have a number where I can reach him?"

"No," Anderson said.

"Well, when you talk to him, ask him to call me. I'll give you my number."

"TM's a busy man," Cooper said. "Do you want to hire him for some canine work?"

"No. I'll tell him why I'm calling when I talk to him."

"Well, it's very unlikely he'll call you back unless he knows why you're calling," Cooper said.

"It's about a murder investigation. The victim's cell phone showed he'd been sending text messages to TM and calling him."

"Who was the victim?" Anderson asked.

"A guy named Daniel Webster," Barrett replied.

"Was he an attorney?" Anderson asked.

"Yes. Why do you ask? Do you know him?"

"Please excuse us for a few moments," Cooper said. "Stay on the line, and we'll be back to you shortly."

"I don't understand," Barrett said. "Why can't you just tell me what you know?"

"We need to check on something," Cooper said. "Just be patient."

Cooper and Anderson left the conference room and went outside the building.

"You asked whether the victim was an attorney," Cooper said. "Do you know him?"

"Yes. He was the lawyer for the kidnap victim's father and the one who hired us. He was TM's contact. I don't believe TM ever talked to the victim's father."

"This is too much of a coincidence," Cooper said. "TM's being chased by people who want to kill the kidnapping victim and now the lawyer has been killed. I think we should talk to this police officer and tell him what we know. TM couldn't have murdered Webster because he was in Costa Rica. But I don't want to talk to him about this on the phone."

OK," Anderson said. "Let's tell him he needs to come here and talk to us in person."

"We're back," Cooper said when she and Anderson returned to the conference room. "We may have some information for you, but we can't talk about it on the phone. You need to come here."

"Why?" Barrett asked. "Why can't you tell me what you know?"

"You say you're a police officer, but we don't know that," Cooper said. "We need to see your identification before we share what might be very sensitive information with you. By the way, I'm a friend of TM and not one of his co-workers. I'm an investigator with the Arizona Department of Safety, but you can't take my word for it because you can't see my identification."

"Where are you located?"

"A few miles outside of Boulder in the foothills of the Rocky Mountains."

"I'll check with my chief and see whether I can come and if so, when," Barrett said reluctantly.

"That's fine," Anderson said. "But you need to be here when Carson is here."

Turning to Anderson, Cooper said, "Would it be possible for us to meet in Phoenix?"

Anderson hesitated and then said, "It's possible, but in that case, Sergeant, you should plan to meet with us early next week."

"The flight would be pretty expensive booked on such short notice. I'll check with the chief and get back to you."

"Like today," Cooper said, not as a question.

"We don't have any choice," the chief said after hearing Barrett's account of the conversation. "As you well know, we're at a dead end and have no clues to work on other than Webster's text messages to this TM. You better meet with them as soon as possible."

38

The 1962 Beechcraft E50 Twin Bonanza bounced hard as it landed on the small runway near La Fortuna. It taxied to a tiny building just to the left of the small terminal and cut the engines. It was not easy for Jesse Crimp to bend down and make his way out of the plane's small door to the single step and then to the pavement. Crimp was six feet five and weighed 260 pounds. He was an imposing figure with his shaved head, short white facial hair, and numerous tattoos. But it was even more difficult for Marty Regus. Although at six feet he was shorter than Crimp, he weighed over 300 pounds, and much of it was fat. His chunky face was partly hidden by his thick, brown, shoulder-length hair. Next was the man the other two called the Professor, Dale Trigent. Trigent, six feet tall and 200 pounds, had deep-set eyes, blond hair with a blond mustache, and an ever-present skullcap. He wore a small diamond earring in his pierced right ear.

The Professor had arranged for a vehicle to be available for them at the airport. He had no idea what kind it would be. It turned out to be a gray four-door 1991 Chevrolet S-10 Blazer. Trident and Regus began to load their bags and equipment into the back of the Blazer. The equipment included two Heckler & Koch PSG1 sniper rifles with Hensoldt telescopic sights, two AK-47s, and three Glock 17 handguns together with ammunition for each of the weapons.

Crimp, Regus, and Trigent referred to themselves as the Trio. They had fought together as marines in Iraq shortly after the invasion, when Regus was far less heavy. The Trio saw many deaths, including some for which they were responsible. They did not always distinguish between friend and foe.

Their lives changed when one day they met a former marine who was working under contract for a government agency. They were startled to learn how much he was paid and the relatively independent life he was able to lead. The Professor went into action and found a way for the three of them to enjoy the same life. He located the head of one of the companies who supplied contract workers to US government agencies and convinced him that the Trio would be a great addition to his contract work force. It was not too difficult to arrange for them to be discharged from the Marine Corps and become contract workers since the Pentagon and White House were anxious to minimize the total number of troops publicly reported to be in Iraq and the media paid little attention to the increased number of contract workers.

The Trio enjoyed their contract pay and status but then got greedy. They discovered they could make even more money by working with corrupt Iraqi officials. If an official found a rival to be standing in his way, he could count on the Trio to eliminate the rival for a handsome fee. Unfortunately for the Trio, they accepted an assignment from an official whose rival was more powerful and was fully aware of what the Trio was up to. He went to the head of the company and told him that if the Trio were not gone within twenty-four hours, he would expose what they had been doing to the appropriate government officials. They were put on a plane within minutes.

Once the Trio were in La Fortuna, the Professor wasted no time in giving instructions. They were to fan out and find out where TM and the girl had gone. He found local people who, for a fee, were only too willing to act as interpreters and seek out locals who could provide useful information.

Natalie thought the ride would never end. Instead of stopping for lunch, she was told to stay on her horse and was given a hard roll with some sort of sausage inside and a bottle of water. When she complained that she needed to go to the bathroom, they finally stopped.

When Natalie returned to her horse, she turned to TM and said, "Do you have any idea where we're going?"

"The guide is taking us south around the volcano and then we'll head northwest next to a lake called Arenal," TM said. "We'll ride along the side of Lake Arenal until we get to a small town called Mata de Canan."

"What do we do when we get there?"

"It's very close to a road that will take us to the Pan-American Highway."

"But we don't have a car. How do we get anywhere?"

"We'll have to figure that out when we get to Mata de Canan."

"That doesn't give me much comfort," Natalie said.

They continued on for what seemed to Natalie to be several more hours until they came to Lake Arenal and the guide signaled they would stop for the evening.

"The first thing we do is water and feed the horses," the guide said. "And then we'll have some dinner and rest for the night."

TM helped the guide unload the two packhorses the guide had brought with them. Dinner consisted of the same rolls and sausage they had had for lunch, but they each had a banana for dessert.

"What do we sleep on?" Natalie asked.

"This," the guide said as he threw her a light sleeping bag. "Pull it up close at the head so the vampire bats don't get you," he said as he turned to TM and grinned.

"Vampire bats!" Natalie screamed. "What do you mean?"

"Oh, didn't you know?" the guide said. "Costa Rica has vampire bats. They cut a hole in the skin and then lap out your blood. But it's not painful."

"No, no," Natalie shrieked. "How can I sleep with that news?"

"The good news is they mainly go after cattle and not humans, so you should be OK," the guide said as he smirked at TM.

39

Feliz Montero had just finished telling Norm Rogers what Montero knew about the confrontation that had taken place at the nearby hotel when Rogers's phone rang. Rogers stopped taking notes and looked down to see who it was.

"Please excuse me while I take this call," he said.

He stepped outside but returned to the room after just a few minutes.

"I won't take any more of your time," Rogers said with a puzzled look on his face. "I was told not to pursue this further."

"But I was told this guy TM is on the very highest list of terrorists," Montero's assistant said loudly.

"All I can say is that, for whatever reason, I was told not to pursue this further. I appreciate your taking the time to see me and sharing information with me. You are to be complimented on the thoroughness of your investigation."

As he drove back to San Jose, Rogers thought about the strange call he had received. No reason was given for the order to discontinue his assignment. In his experience, this was most unusual, and his superior had almost seemed embarrassed when he gave the order. Rogers always tried to keep up to date with people on the highest list of terrorists and was not aware of TM being on the list until he was told to pursue him. And that order came after the hotel incident.

Montero's account of the incident indicated that people were trying to kill TM and whoever was with him. Who would be trying to kill him if he was a terrorist? The most likely people would be from Special Operations, but these people would not have failed. TM would be dead. He wondered what this TM person was all about. He decided to find out more about him, but the best way to do that was to talk to some friends at the agency. He knew that, given the order he had received, it would not be a good idea for him to pursue it himself.

"I don't see how this is something that involves Arizona," the head of Arizona's Department of Public Safety said to Cooper.

"Well, it really all started here," Cooper said. "The girl was a student in Flagstaff before she went missing and TM was working here before he went after her in Costa Rica. If there's any state that has a relationship to this, it's Arizona."

"Are either of them Arizona residents?"

"The girl probably is because she was living here."

"Come on, Carson, just because she was a student here doesn't mean she's an Arizona resident. And if both of them are in Costa Rica, what can we do?"

"We can make sure that someone in the United States is looking after their interests. You took a chance when you sent me to work with TM to find the Flagstaff killer, and because of that he's been found and put behind bars."

The DPS head sat silent for a few moments. "It's very tenuous. But I'll let you work on this with one condition."

"What's that?"

"You don't do anything to embarrass DPS."

"Oh. Of course not," a smiling Cooper said and quickly left the head's office.

The planes carrying Anderson and Sergeant Barrett landed at Phoenix Sky Harbor airport within a few minutes of each other, and both deplaned passengers at Terminal Four, where Cooper was waiting for them. A short drive later they were at DPS headquarters in Phoenix, where Cooper had reserved a conference room.

Anderson described how he and TM had been hired to use dogs to search a portion of the Coconino National Forest because of the possibility that the client's daughter had been buried there as a victim of a serial killer.

"Webster was the person who hired TM and was our only contact with the client, whom we never met. At a certain point Webster frantically contacted TM and said the client had received a call that his daughter had been kidnapped. A few days later, Webster said the daughter was being held for ransom in San Jose, Costa Rica. He begged TM to go there, pay the ransom, and rescue the daughter. TM reluctantly agreed. Three days later I got a text message that he had been successful. But a few days later I got a phone call from TM that still sends shivers down my spine. He said the police were looking for him because there had been some bad incidents and they thought he was a criminal."

"This fits with what we found on Webster's cell phone," Barrett said. "There were a couple of text messages from TM that must have been around that time. One said that the package had arrived. What package could he have been talking about?"

"That probably was the ransom. It was a million-dollar gold bearer bond. TM didn't want to carry it with him, so it was sent to him by courier in San Jose."

"The other text message was about the same as the one you received. That he had been successful. So the key question is what happened after that. Have you heard from him since the chilling phone call you described?"

"No, but I've received calls from law enforcement people in Costa Rica asking for TM."

"What did they say?" Barrett asked.

"I never really talked to them."

"What's the client's name?" "I don't know," Anderson sheepishly said.

"Where does the client live?"

"I don't know. But we did receive payments from him both by check and wire transfer, and maybe you could trace them back and find his identity."

"We'll do that. In the meantime I suggest you talk to the people who called from Costa Rica and find out what they wanted."

"Why don't we do that now?" Cooper asked. "Do you have their numbers?"

"Not with me, but I can call my office and get them."

"When you do that, ask your office to also fax or e-mail whatever they have that can help us trace the funds you received from the client," Barrett said. "While you're doing that, I'll get someone at my place to try to find out the names of Webster's clients. That's not easy because his law firm claims the information is confidential."

"Let's take a break while you make your calls and get back together in thirty minutes," Cooper said.

When they reconvened, they called the first number Anderson had written down. It turned out to be the number for Chief Inspector Roberto Diaz's office. It was not easy to get to talk to someone who was familiar with the call to TM's office. Cooper, who was fluent in Spanish, did the initial talking. They finally got through to one of Diaz's assistants, who described the events that had taken place in San Jose and the reason they were looking for TM.

"Is he there with you?" the assistant asked.

"No, he's not," Anderson replied. "The last we heard from him he said people were trying to kill him."

"Well, they certainly tried here," the assistant said. "Let me see if I can get the chief inspector on the line."

"Who are you?" a loud, authoritative voice said after a brief delay.

"There are three of us," Cooper said. "I'm an investigator with the Arizona Department of Public Safety. Roger Barrett is a sergeant with the Evanston, Illinois, Police Department, and Jim Anderson works for TM. We're calling you because we're trying to locate TM and noticed that you had called his office."

Sergeant Barrett explained that he was a police officer investigating the murder of a lawyer who may have had something to do with the reason TM was in Costa Rica.

"What was the reason?" Diaz asked.

"TM was hired by the murdered lawyer to deliver a ransom for a girl who was kidnapped and taken to San Jose by the kidnapper," Anderson said. "He notified us that he had been successful in rescuing her but later called and said people were trying to kill her and were after him as well. He said the police were looking for him."

"Where was he when he called?" Diaz asked.

"He must have been in La Fortuna because he had me wire funds to a bank there," Anderson replied.

"Have you tried to call him?"

"He told me he can't use his cell phone because the killers are using that to track him. He called me with a new cell phone he said he bought, but he doesn't answer when I call him at the new number. He must have it turned off."

"He was right about people trying to kill the girl and him," Diaz said. "They fired shots at a vehicle he was driving, and this led to a shootout that killed one of my men. Do you know where he went to deliver the ransom?"

"It was the office of Rand Trading Company. I don't have the address with me," Anderson said.

"We'll find it. Hold on."

They could hear Diaz shouting to one of his assistants. A few minutes later he came back on the phone. "We found the address, and I'm sending men there now. Give me your telephone number and I'll call you back as soon as I get a report."

"Our office had a call from another number in Costa Rica," Anderson said and gave Diaz the number.

"That doesn't sound familiar. I'll check on that too," Diaz said and hung up.

"Has anything come in from your office about the money TM received?" Barrett asked Anderson.

"I have an e-mail with some attachments," Anderson said.

"Follow me," Cooper said, "and I'll find a printer for you to use."

When Cooper and Anderson returned, Anderson handed Barrett a copy of a check written on an account in the name of J.T. and J.F. Morgan Family Trust with a Kenilworth, Illinois, address.

"I'll call my office and have them locate the Morgans," Barrett said.

40

The Professor's plan worked. Two local people reported that TM and the girl had left on horseback in the direction of Lake Arenal. He met with Crimp and Regus at a table in the back of a quiet fast food restaurant and spread a map of the area out on the table.

"They've been gone too long for us to have any chance to catch up with them, so we have to plan to find them when their ride ends. From what I was told, most horseback riding begins and ends near here in La Fortuna, but they must be going farther. They'll be next to Lake Arenal for quite a ways, and the closest place for them to end their ride and be in any kind of a populated area is the very small town of Mata de Canan. I've marked the location of the town on the map."

"That's quite a ways from here," Jesse said.

"That's why we have the Blazer. My idea is that Jesse and I will set up with our scope rifles about a hundred yards from the likely place where the two will come into town."

"What about me?" Regus asked.

"You'll be in the Blazer closer to the target area. If either of them is still alive, you'll finish them off. Also, we need proof that the two are dead, so you'll photograph the bodies. That way we should have no trouble getting the bonus we were promised for being successful. Of course all of this makes sense on paper, but we'll have to set the specific locations when we get there."

"When do we go to this town you mentioned?" Jesse asked.

"I think we have time to sleep here tonight and set out in the morning," the Professor said.

"Where will we stay?" Crimp asked.

"At some place that has beds," the Professor replied sarcastically.

"Did you sleep all right?" TM asked.

"Of course not," Natalie replied. "I was scared to death bats would come. I don't think I slept a wink. How long will it take us to get to the town you talked about?"

"The guide said we'd be there before dark."

"Do you still have the guns?"

"You keep asking me that. I have both of them. Do you want one?"

"No way," Natalie shouted. "I'd probably shoot myself. My mother must be frantic by this time wondering where we are. Could I use the phone to call her?"

"No. We could have the same problem as before where people would use it to track us. I wouldn't be at all surprised if the people trying to kill us are monitoring your parents' phone lines. I might call my office at some point, but I'm concerned about that being traced as well. These people seem to be very sophisticated technically."

"I wonder if my father knows people are trying to kill us. It's obvious he told someone when he heard Ken say the word *Sage.* You know how I feel about my father, but I can't believe he would want people to kill me. He knows how much that would hurt my mother, and he loves her too much to be part of trying to kill me."

"Do you know who the top person is in this group?"

"No. But I'm sure he's in New York."

"I thought you said Ken knew the people involved."

"He knew many of them, but he never told me who he thought was the leader. Have you given any more thought to how we get out of the country?"

"I told you. We'll try to find a way to get to the Pan-American Highway and take that north across the border."

"Do you have enough money to buy a car?"

"No. Not even close to enough."

"Maybe we can steal one."

"No thanks. I don't want even more police searching for us. Hopefully I have enough money to hire someone to drive us across the border."

"Maybe we should have kept the car we stole at the hotel where you killed two of the bad guys."

"I'm sure the police would have been looking for that car so that would not have been an option."

"I don't know how I'm gonna make it today. My legs and butt are sore and I'm tired because of no sleep."

"You'll find a way."

41

The information Rogers received from his friends at Langley had him even more perplexed. Not only had they not found anything linking TM to any kind of terrorists, but they had also discovered that he had worked in the past for the Drug Enforcement Agency as an undercover agent. Notwithstanding this, they confirmed that TM was on a special list that was accessible only to the most senior agency officials. They warned Rogers that it did not behoove him to spend any more time thinking about TM.

Barrett was reporting to Cooper and Anderson what Barrett's office had learned about the Morgans when a call came in from Diaz.

"We learned a lot," Diaz said. "Two bodies were found at the offices of Rand Trading Company. One of them was an American named Kenneth Alexander. The other was the manager of Rand Trading Company. The American had been tortured; it looks as though his killers were seeking information from him. It's likely they were successful. They must have found out where TM and the woman were staying, which is what led to the encounter where one of our people was killed. There's more. TM and the woman were attacked at a hotel in San Ramon. The body of one of the attackers was found in their hotel room and another was found just outside the hotel. It gets more bizarre. Our bureau office that investigated has a man with a friend at your Homeland Security. He was told that TM is on the highest list of terrorists."

"*What?*" Cooper and Anderson shouted in unison.

"Yes. An agent from your counterterrorism agency met with the bureau people, but it was very strange."

"How so?" Barrett asked.

"While he was in the meeting he got a phone call that he went outside to take. When he returned, he said he was told not to get further involved and left."

"This makes absolutely no sense," Cooper said. "There's no way TM could be a terrorist. Do you have the agent's name?"

"Norman Rogers. It wasn't easy, but I got his phone number. When I called him, he refused to talk to me about the matter."

"Can you help us find TM?" Anderson asked.

"Of course. But it won't be easy. You said he had you wire money to a bank in La Fortuna. E-mail me a detailed description of TM, and I'll alert our people to be looking for him."

When the Trio arrived in Mata de Canan, they found some adjustments to the plan were necessary. The places where the Professor and Jesse originally intended to set up their sniper rifles were too visible, which made it necessary to move several yards farther back where there was some concealment. The range would now be closer to one hundred and fifty yards rather than one hundred. Conversely, they found an inconspicuous place where Regus could park the Blazer and quickly get to where he could photograph the bodies. Each of them had a two-way radio with an earpiece that also had a voice-activated microphone.

The Trio waited patiently for their prey. The Professor and Jesse were able to set up their rifles and adjust the sights to the desired distance. They also adjusted for the light prevailing wind. The Professor told Jesse that he would take out the girl and Jesse was to take out the man. Several hours passed with people walking in both directions along the route the man and the girl were expected to take. But there was no sign of them.

Suddenly the Professor quietly said, "Here they come. Wait for my command."

But TM and Natalie were not cooperating. Instead of walking side by side, TM was walking a few feet in front of Natalie, and only about half of Natalie could be viewed in the sight of the Professor's rifle. He decided to take his chances.

"Get ready. Fire on three. One, two, three."

But at that moment, for whatever reason, TM turned to his left, and both bullets hit Natalie, who dropped to the ground. TM immediately ducked and ran for cover behind a small wall. Both the Professor and Jesse fired several shots at TM but missed.

"Get him, Regus!" the Professor shouted into his radio.

Regus floored the Blazer and raced to the area where he had last seen TM. He grabbed his Glock, pulled his heavy body out of the car, and ducked behind the front of the car while he tried to locate TM. He saw sudden movement and rose up slightly to aim his Glock in that direction.

But the movement was not TM. It was a branch that TM had thrown from several feet away. As Regus turned toward the movement, TM rose and fired one shot from his Wilson .45 that struck Regus in the temple. TM jumped over the wall and climbed in the driver's seat of the Blazer, which was still running. He circled the Blazer and came to a stop with the driver's side next to Natalie's body. As bullets struck the Blazer, TM lifted Natalie and placed her body on the floor in front of the passenger seat. He then jumped back in the driver's seat and kept his head low as he floored the Blazer and drove away as more bullets struck the vehicle.

The Professor and Jesse had begun running toward Regus as soon as they saw TM had not been hit. When they saw that Regus had been shot, they fired their sniper rifles at the Blazer, but their accuracy from a standing position was far worse than when they were in a prone position, and none of the bullets hit TM.

"We're screwed," the Professor said as he stood next to Regus's body. "Regus is dead, and we lost the Blazer. I think I killed the girl, but we don't have a body to prove it."

"What do we do now?" Jesse asked.

"We need to get away from here as fast as we can before the police come. We may have to ditch the sniper rifles because we stick out like a sore thumb carrying them around. One way or another, we need to get a vehicle. The man is going to take the girl to a medical facility, and hopefully we can catch up with him there. We still have our Glocks. If he ditches the Blazer, we may be able to get the AK-47s, but that's unlikely."

42

When Sergeant Barrett returned to Evanston, he made plans to interview Jeffrey Morgan. It was clear from what he had learned from Anderson and Cooper that Morgan was a client of Webster's and not just a minor one. Barrett's office had learned that Morgan's wife had recently committed suicide. And of course he knew that Morgan's daughter had been kidnapped and rescued by TM. He doubted whether all of this was just a coincidence.

But they had no grounds to take Morgan into custody. He had no obligation to talk to them, and if he didn't, there wasn't much they could do. Barrett decided he would try to interview Morgan at his home. Even though it was office policy to have two people do an interview, he decided to go by himself because that would be less intimidating. He picked late afternoon for his attempted interview because the main financial markets would be closed then and Morgan would seemingly be more available. He went to the front door, pushed the button for the doorbell, and was somewhat startled when Morgan appeared at the door.

"Mr. Morgan, I'm Sergeant Barrett from the Evanston Police Department," he said as he presented his badge and ID. "We're investigating the murder of your attorney, Daniel Webster, and I was hoping you could help us find his killer."

Morgan hesitated. The last thing he wanted was to talk to Barrett. But the way Barrett presented his request made it difficult to refuse. It would appear strange if he didn't want to help find Webster's killer.

"I don't think I have much to contribute," Morgan said.

"Sometimes little things can be very meaningful," Barrett said. "I won't take much of your time. Can I come in?"

"OK," Morgan said reluctantly, "but I don't have much time."

Morgan led Barrett through a marble-floored entryway to a sunken living room that featured a beamed cathedral ceiling, carved stone fireplace, oriental rugs, and antique French furniture. Morgan offered Barrett a seat in a red velvet sofa and sat opposite him in a high-backed wing chair.

Barrett wasted no time getting to the point. "We understand Webster was working on the kidnapping of your daughter. Do you have any idea who was responsible?"

"No," Morgan snapped, startled. "I wish I did."

"I understand she was rescued by a man Webster hired and is safe. Is she home yet?"

"No. But I'm very relieved she's safe."

"When do you expect her?"

"I'm not sure."

"Have you talked to her lately?"

"Not for a few days."

"How do you know she's safe?"

"Because she called after she was freed. You have to understand. Natalie is a very independent person, and it's not at all surprising that she didn't rush home."

"Do you know how to reach her?"

"No. She had a cell phone, but apparently that was lost when she was kidnapped."

"Did she say anything about the kidnapper when she called?"

"No."

"Here's my card. Please let me know if you hear from her. I'd like to talk to her."

Morgan did not respond.

As Barrett got up to leave, he turned to Morgan and said, "I was sorry to hear about your wife."

Barrett thought he saw a look of fear in Morgan's eyes.

"Are you sure *you* are safe?" Barrett asked.

43

TM was stunned. After all he and Natalie had been through, it was unbelievable that she had been shot. As he drove away from the shooting scene, he frantically looked for some sign of a hospital or clinic. She had seemed lifeless when he put her in the Blazer, but maybe she was still alive and could be saved if he could get medical help. The Blazer was showing the effects of the bullets that had been fired into it. Its engine was periodically coughing, and the temperature gauge was in the red area.

TM had driven a few miles when he came to the town of Nueva Arenal. Much of the original town of Arenal was destroyed by an eruption of the Arenal volcano in 1968, and the rest was destroyed when Lake Arenal was created in 1973. TM spotted a sign for what appeared to be a small clinic. He drove to the front of the clinic, lifted Natalie out of the Blazer, and carried her into the clinic. He walked past startled people in the waiting room and straight into an examining room where there was an empty gurney.

Without a word, a doctor in the room went to Natalie and checked for signs of life. Within moments, he rose and shook his head.

"I'm sorry about your wife," the doctor said in perfect English.

"She wasn't my wife," TM replied, "but someone I was trying to protect. We came a long way, and I'm devastated this happened."

"Who shot her?"

"I don't know. People have tried several times to kill her, and now they've succeeded. They tried to kill me as well. They know I'd take her to a health facility and could well come here looking for me. The Blazer I came in is dying, and I need some form of transportation."

"I can't help you. Do you have any money?"

"Some."

"There is a man in the waiting room who has an old motor scooter. If you pay him the right price, I think he'll sell it to you."

"Will you help me?"

TM and the doctor went through the waiting room and found the scooter leaning against the building. It was a Honda.

"You're right. It's old," TM said.

"But I think it's been maintained," the doctor said, "and it runs pretty good."

"I don't have any choice. Let's get it done."

After some give and take, TM was able to buy the motor scooter for what he considered a very rich price.

When they were back in the examining room, TM asked the doctor whether he could use a phone to call someone in the United States. "I still have some money left and can pay you for using the phone."

"That won't be necessary. I'll take you to my office."

"What will happen to the body?" TM asked.

"I'll call the police, and they will take it to a mortuary in La Fortuna that serves as the local morgue. Will you contact her next of kin?"

"No, for reasons I can't get into. She has identification on her body that the police can use to contact someone."

The phone rang for what seemed like forever before TM finally heard Anderson's voice.

"It's TM, Anderson."

"Cooper is here. Let me put you on the speakerphone."

"Natalie has been shot and is dead," TM said.

"How did that happen?" Cooper asked.

"We rode horses on a trail that I thought would let us escape from the people who were after us. But they figured out where we would be when the trail ended and were waiting for us. Apparently they had sniper rifles, because I didn't see the gunmen before they fired. It's a miracle I'm still alive. I turned slightly when they fired, and the bullet meant for me probably hit Natalie, although she was struck by another bullet that probably was fatal."

"Where are you now?" Anderson asked.

"In a town called Nuevo Arenal, which isn't far from La Fortuna, where you wired the money."

"Stay there!" Cooper exclaimed. "We've been in touch with the top law enforcement officer in San Jose, and he'll send his men there to get you to a safe place."

"Won't work," TM said. "It would take too long for them to get here, and the killers will probably be here soon. I need to get out of here."

"Things are worse than you think," Cooper said. "You're on a list of top terrorists and will be apprehended when you enter the United States. We have no idea how this happened."

"Unbelievable," TM said. "The kidnapping was a sham. Natalie and her boyfriend wanted to get money out of Natalie's stepfather,

Jeffrey Morgan. The boyfriend knew Morgan was part of a ring of powerful people who use sophisticated methods to hide insider trading. Apparently there was a code word used by the ring, and the boyfriend, out of frustration with Morgan's delaying tactics, shouted it out during a ransom phone call. Morgan must have panicked and reported it to the head of the ring. That was a death warrant for the boyfriend and Natalie. And because I rescued Natalie, I'm a target as well."

"But you don't know the identity of the members of the ring," Anderson said.

"I know one of them, Jeffrey Morgan."

"You should know that Webster was murdered," Anderson said. "That probably was a reaction as well."

"And Morgan's wife committed suicide," Cooper said. "Or at least that's what was reported."

"These people are incredibly dangerous and have tentacles in the highest levels of government," TM said. "So high that they were able to get me on the terrorist list. I'm going to need your help. I have to get away from the killers or do away with them and then find a way to get back into the States."

"We need to get you some place where Chief Inspector Diaz and his men can protect you," Cooper said. "Do you have a car?"

"No, but I just overpaid for an old motor scooter."

"Where are you planning to go?" Cooper asked.

"I was planning to get to the Pan-American Highway where I would head north and either drive into Nicaragua or head for the coast and try to get a boat to take me north. I'm going to start out on back roads so there's less chance of the killers finding me. I don't know how you will ever find me."

"We'll have to find a way," Cooper said. "What are you wearing?"

"A dirty blue shirt and dirty jeans."

"Hopefully we won't have to smell you until you've had a shower," Cooper said.

"There's something very, very important," TM said.

"What's that?" Anderson asked.

"Making sure Morgan stays alive. He's the one person we know who can bring down the ring. Everything else now is hearsay or circumstantial evidence."

"There is one thing much more important," Cooper said. "Keeping you alive. You better be going."

As he left the clinic, TM thought it best to move the Blazer to a less conspicuous place. But the Blazer had died and would not start. TM opened the rear door and saw the two AK-47s and several boxes of ammunition. He removed the AK-47s and smashed both of them against a concrete pillar.

After Anderson and Cooper hung up from TM, they made two calls. The first was to Chief Inspector Diaz and lasted several minutes. The second was to Sergeant Barrett.

"I never would have imagined a murder case could get so bizarre," Barrett said after Anderson and Cooper had described their conversation with TM. "It won't be easy to keep Morgan alive if someone is really after him. We have no grounds to take him into custody, and he doesn't live in my jurisdiction. The Kenilworth police chief is an old friend of mine and I can confide in him, but the insider trading aspect is so sensitive that it has to be kept confidential from everyone else. I don't think I can even tell the mayor about it.

"Morgan really needs bodyguards, but the closest we can come is to have officers doing surveillance. Somehow I have to convince the mayor that Morgan is an important material witness so he'll let me use our people for surveillance. Have you figured out a way to get TM?"

"We're working on it," Cooper said.

44

The Professor and Jesse walked for what seemed to Jesse to be forever. But the Professor was thinking all the while. They obviously needed a vehicle. One option was to steal one. They could flag down a car, kill the driver, and drive away. But this was easier said than done. Further, it would draw even more police attention to the area. The Professor had tried to plan for all eventualities. So far his planning had not been very successful with one exception. He had substantial amounts of money.

After some inquiries, they were able to find someone who would drive for hire. His name was Berto Raiss, and he had a 2010 Chevrolet Impala that appeared to be in excellent condition. For appearances' sake, the Professor bargained hard with Raiss but agreed to an amount that he knew Raiss would find very acceptable.

Raiss's first assignment was to take the Professor and Jesse to the nearest clinic or hospital. There was only one, and soon they were at the clinic that TM had left only minutes before.

"There's the Blazer," Jesse shouted.

"See if it works," the Professor replied, "while I find out what happened here."

There were four people in the waiting room and a woman behind a desk who took care of the appointments. She was anything but friendly, but the Professor alternated charm with flattery to ingratiate himself with her.

"Why do you need to see the doctor?" the woman asked.

"I've been having pains in my shoulder," the Professor said. "But I can certainly wait my turn with the others. It must get boring dealing with sick people. I'll bet nothing much happens to relieve the boredom."

"Oh. We had some excitement earlier today."

"What happened?"

"A man came in with the body of a woman who had been shot."

"Was the doctor able to save her?"

"No. She was dead already."

"That's terrible," the Professor said. "What happened to the man?"

"He said people were trying to kill him too, and he left."

"Good. He drove away in his car?"

"Oh no. His car was hit with bullets and wouldn't start so he bought a motor scooter and drove away."

"I'm so glad. Did he say where he was going?"

"Not to me."

Jesse was standing next to Raiss's car when the Professor left the clinic. "The Blazer's dead," Jesse said.

"That's what I learned in the clinic. He drove away on a motor scooter."

"Oh shit!" Jesse exclaimed. "How will we ever find him? There are several roads he can take, and it would be a miracle if we were on the same one as him."

"Excuse me," Raiss said quietly.

"Shut up," Jesse shouted. "We're trying to figure out what to do."

The Professor put up his hand, turned to Raiss, and softly said, "What did you want to say?"

"I can help you find him."

"How?" the Professor asked.

"Facebook. I have a lot of friends in the area on Facebook. I can post a message for them to respond to me as soon as possible if they see a man passing through on a motor scooter."

"How would that help?" Jesse asked. "There must be a lot of people driving on a motor scooter."

"Yes, but someone here told me he wasn't wearing a helmet. Everyone here wears a helmet. I'll have them look for someone who isn't wearing a helmet."

"Do it," the Professor exclaimed. "Jesse, were there any guns in the Blazer?"

"No, just ammunition."

"All we have is our Glocks, which isn't enough."

"Maybe I can help," Raiss said. "What would you like?"

"Preferably AK-47s," the Professor replied. "Because we have ammunition for them."

"I'll find a way," Raiss said. "But it won't be cheap."

"I'm sure you'll be reasonable," the Professor said, "and we'll come up with the money."

45

"It's confirmed," Cragin said. "The girl is dead."

"Great," Bertre said. "What about the man who rescued her?"

"He got away."

"Damn! How did that happen?"

"He was lucky. But he doesn't know that much anyway. Maybe we would be better off forgetting about him."

"Absolutely not! You can be sure the girl told him everything she knew. He's also a link to Morgan and Webster. Keep after him. It's urgent."

"I wonder how Morgan will deal with the death of his daughter," Cragin said.

"She wasn't his real daughter, so it probably won't hit him very hard, and he knew we were looking for her. I'll tell him to have her cremated and not to have any memorial or other service that would draw attention to her death."

"Maybe it's time for Morgan to go?

"No, for a couple of reasons," Bertre said. "He's part of our circle and other people will get nervous if we do something to him. Also, with the death of his wife and Webster, his death would raise a big red flag, particularly if any word gets out about his daughter.

But we'll have to keep a close eye on him. I'll find a way to get him an assistant who can watch him for us."

Morgan did not take the news of Natalie's death as well as Bertre thought. She wasn't his biological daughter and they had had many arguments, but he knew how much his wife had adored Natalie. And he was overwhelmed by all that had happened. First the death of his lawyer Webster, then the loss of his wife and now the death of Natalie. All of this was not happening in a vacuum. He didn't know if TM was still alive, and if he was, whether he knew anything at all about Sage. And then there was the visit from the Evanston police sergeant and his final words: "Are you sure *you* are safe?"

No. He wasn't sure he was safe. If Bertre could arrange all these deaths, he could easily arrange to kill him. So what should he do? Going to the police and exposing Sage was out of the question. Although unlikely, he couldn't be sure Sage hadn't corrupted the people he talked to. And if they hadn't, he surely would wind up in prison.

He decided there was one thing he could do to protect himself from Bertre. He would make a recording where he would reveal everything about Sage and place the recording in a safe deposit box with instructions to turn the recording over to the FBI if anything happened to him. He would then tell Bertre what he had done. Bertre would not be happy, but there wasn't much he could do.

46

There was no nonstop flight from Phoenix to San Jose, so Carson Cooper flew on United Airlines to Houston, where she caught a flight to San Jose. With her hair in a bun and her wire-rimmed glasses, she looked as inconspicuous as when TM met her in Flagstaff. There was a long line at immigration, and when she finally passed through into the baggage claim area, there was a large crowd waiting for passengers. She looked around and noticed two men in police uniforms with one of them holding a small sign that read *Cooper.* She approached the one with the sign.

"Miss Cooper?" he asked.

"Yes," she responded.

"I am Officer Resto, and this is Officer Westorso. We are from OIJ. Chief Inspector Diaz assigned us to work with you while you are in our country."

"Did he tell you what we need to do?"

"He said we must find a man called TM who is being pursued by people who want to kill him."

"Did he tell you how we hope to find him?"

"Only that he would be headed north on the Pan-American Highway and that you said you would have special equipment that would help us."

"What transportation and equipment do you have with you?"

"Officer Westorso and I will be with you in our car. We also have a van with four heavily armed policemen."

"What about a truck?" Cooper asked.

"We have a large panel truck, which is also parked outside," Resto responded.

"Good. We need to go to the freight terminal to pick up the equipment I sent."

There were seven boxes waiting for Cooper when they arrived at the dock for Airborne Express. Cooper took the smallest box and said she wanted to have that with her in the car. The other boxes were quickly loaded on the panel truck.

"We need to hurry," Cooper said. "Our only hope of finding TM is to get to where he plans to enter the Pan-American Highway before he does."

The traffic was heavy near the airport, but once they got on the Pan-American Highway, the car and van used their sirens and emergency lights to move past the regular traffic. At times they were going so fast that Cooper was beginning to think she had stressed the necessity of speed too much.

While in the back of the car, she opened the small box and took out a GPS unit and two computer tablets. She used one of the tablets to track their progress on a map of the area.

After several minutes, Cooper asked Resto to find a place where they could pull over and have room to work with the boxes in the truck. After a few more miles, Resto slowed the car and led the van and truck into a large open field. The van had a lift gate that enabled the men to lower the boxes to the ground and carry them to a place where they could be opened. In Spanish, Cooper guided the men as they slid equipment out from the boxes and assembled the equipment into two units.

Each unit had four arms connected to what appeared to be a large cartridge with legs leading to struts that formed a base on the ground. At the end of each arm were two rotors positioned about three inches apart.

"What do you call them, and how do they work?" Resto asked.

"They're newly developed helicopter drones," Cooper said. "They have electric motors and are controlled from the tablets I have. Fortunately Arizona is a leader in the development of drones, and I've been working with some of the developers to see what might be the best drone to use by our Department of Public Safety. These drones are much faster than earlier models. They can reach a top speed of sixty miles an hour and can fly as high as ten thousand feet. They can stay in the air for over four hours at a time and have several different kinds of sensors, including GPS, gyros, and magnetometers. They have high-definition video cameras that I can control from the tablet. They can carry guns and missiles, but these aren't armed. They were pre-assembled so we could use them immediately, and I'm going to get them in the air now. Let's get back in the car and van. We can leave the truck here."

Once in the car, Cooper tapped one of her tablets. One of the drones' rotors immediately started to spin, and the drone lifted off into the air. Seconds later she tapped again and the other drone became air bound.

"We'll be able to monitor all the roads leading to the Pan-American Highway," Cooper said.

"But what do we do if we see TM?" Resto asked. "How will he know we're trying to help him?"

"Great question," Cooper replied. "I have something on each of the drones that will let him know. Let's hope it works."

47

TM drove as fast as he could whenever he was on a straight, open road, but he was slowed by trucks and cars in front of him and by sharp curves. On certain stretches, the road was filled with potholes and was very rough. This slowed his progress considerably. He took more chances than he would have liked in passing vehicles and had more than one close call. He had debated whether to take a circuitous route or go as directly as he could to the Pan-American Highway. He had decided to go directly partly because he wasn't sure where the various other roads went.

He was making what he thought was good progress until it started to rain heavily and he was forced to pull over to the side of the road and take shelter under a tree. The storm lasted more than two hours and then, thoroughly soaked, he proceeded on his way.

True to his word, Raiss took the Professor and Jesse to people who could sell them two AK-47s. Raiss told them the guns were five thousand dollars each. The Professor was sure Raiss would keep much of the money, so he didn't complain. The time would come when they would get some of it back. The trip to buy the guns took them somewhat out of the way, but Raiss had some good news.

"My Facebook friends have spotted the man, and he seems to be taking one road that leads to the Pan-American Highway," Raiss said.

"How far ahead is he?" The Professor asked.

"Probably about six kilometers."

"Can we catch up with him?"

"With any other driver, no. With me, yes."

"How long will it take?"

"At least a couple of hours. Unless he rides motor scooters a lot, he probably will slow down more than necessary at curves, and I'm better at passing other cars."

"Better than someone on a motor scooter?"

"Much better, because when necessary I use my special weapon."

"What's that?"

"Intimidation."

"Intimidation?"

"I honk my horn and flash my lights, and if that doesn't do it, I bump them."

"What are you seeing?" Resto asked Cooper.

"I'm still trying to get acclimated," Cooper replied. "It doesn't help that there are clouds in the area. I have one of the drones at five thousand feet and the other at about one thousand. I'll move the tablets so you can see them. You know the area, and I need your help to focus on the right places."

"I'd bring the higher one down a little lower and move it toward the northeast. Is that the lower one we're seeing?"

"Sure looks like it," Cooper replied.

"How will you be able to pick out TM? There surely are other men riding motor scooters."

"Once we see someone on a motor scooter we'll zoom down and take a closer look."

"Are you pretty familiar with TM's appearance?" Resto asked.

"I think so," Cooper replied, keeping to herself what she was really thinking.

TM accelerated as he came to a place where the traffic had thinned out and the road was straight. As far as he could tell, he was only a few miles away from the Pan-American Highway. He was still unsure about what he would do when he got there. He didn't know if he was still being pursued and if he was, whether his pursuers were very close. He was hopeful he could find a place where he could get out of his wet clothes and change into the dry clothes in his backpack. Cooper had said that a police official from San Jose would send men to help him. Once he got to the Pan-American Highway, he would try to find a phone to call Jim or Cooper and tell them where he was.

Traffic started to build, and TM was forced to slow down. It was hard to hear over the sound of his scooter's motor, but TM thought he heard a lot of honking coming from behind him. Suddenly he heard bullets whistling past him. And if that wasn't bad enough, he was astonished to see a craft of some sort hovering a few feet above and ahead of him. He couldn't believe it. People shooting at him from behind and now there was this craft above him that he expected any moment to fire a missile or something similar at him.

He could not have anticipated what happened next. A small, weighted banner rolled down from the bottom of the craft with letters he could easily read.

COOPER

Outstanding, he thought to himself. But he still had the shooters from behind to deal with.

TM couldn't see it, but the other drone was above and slightly ahead of Raiss's car moving at the same speed. And no one in the car below knew the drone was there either. But that changed when the drone dropped a plastic ball, no more than twelve inches in diameter, that landed on Raiss's windshield and splattered a black substance across the glass.

"I can't see!" Raiss screamed as his car veered off the road, hit a ditch, and overturned.

TM heard the crash behind him and knew immediately that Cooper had worked her magic. The drone above and in front of him rocked back and forth as though to brag about what it and its sibling had accomplished.

The drone led TM to a place off the road where he saw a group of armed policemen, a van, and a car. He drove the motor scooter to the car and watched as two drones settled down in an adjacent field. The right rear passenger door opened, and Cooper stepped out, beaming. He stepped off the cycle and hugged her.

"You did it again," he said softly. "You saved my life."

"You would have found a way," she said. "I just gave you a hand. As much as I liked that hug, you don't smell very good. We're very near the Pan-American Highway and there's a small hotel close by. I'd ask you to ride in the car, but not with the smell. Follow us on your motor scooter."

The hotel was small, but it had a nice room with a shower. TM shed his clothes and tossed them out the door. The shower felt better than any he had had before. But it got better. The bathroom door opened, and Cooper came in. He watched as she took off her clothes and stepped in the shower with him. They embraced and kissed with passion. Soon they were out of the shower, dried each other with towels, and climbed into bed together. He gently probed her body and soon was inside her. With every thrust their breathing intensified until they jointly reached a level of sheer ecstasy and cried out together. Exhausted, they both fell asleep.

Two of the occupants of Raiss's car were not wearing seat belts and died in the crash. The other occupant survived virtually unhurt. It was the Professor. The previous purpose of his mission had been to kill the girl and the man and collect a big fee. But now it became even more. His two cohorts were dead, and he was obsessed with revenge. He had to locate and kill TM.

48

“Where do we go from here?” Cooper asked as they sat in the hotel’s small eating area.

“Great question,” TM replied. “Obviously I need to get back to the States, but you told me I’m on some kind of terrorist list and would be arrested if I went through immigration at any border crossing.”

“Unless and until we expose Sage, you’re going to continue to have that problem. But I don’t see a good way to do that. Do you?”

“I could contact the FBI, but everything I know is hearsay, and the person who told me about Sage is dead.”

“But we do know one person who knows the facts.”

“Morgan,” TM exclaimed, “but he’s not about to reveal them since he would be implicated.”

“Don’t be too sure,” Cooper said. “His lawyer was killed, as was his stepdaughter, even if he didn’t care that much for her. And Barrett said his wife committed suicide recently and that Morgan seemed very tense when Barrett visited him. There is one person who would have a good chance of getting him to talk and that’s you.”

"You're right. I'm not a stranger to him and can bring up facts he would just as soon not have revealed. This makes it all the more important for me to get across the border."

"I never thought I would say this," Cooper said, "but we have to find a way to get you in as if you were an illegal immigrant."

"Ouch. I don't look forward to trying to scale the wall the government put up. There's got to be a better way. Can one of your drones fly me across?"

"Hardly," she said with a laugh. "I have an idea. We have someone here in Costa Rica who has been incredibly helpful. Chief Inspector Diaz. I'll ask him if he has any suggestions."

"What are you going to do with the drones?" TM asked.

"I'll have to get them packed and sent back. People wouldn't be very happy if I didn't return them."

"That means you'll be going back to San Jose and leaving me, which, as much as I would hate to see you go, would be for the best."

"Why do you say that?" a hurt Cooper asked.

"Thanks to you I survived the last attack, but they probably will send someone else to get me and I don't want you to get hurt."

"In case you haven't noticed, I can look after myself. And you are safer with me than without me."

"Why do you say that?"

"You see all the policemen with us? As long as you are with me in Costa Rica they will be with us and you will be safe."

"But San Jose is the wrong direction."

"How do you expect to go anywhere? On the motor scooter all the way to the States? If you come with me to San Jose, we can figure out the best way to get there and will have some resources to help us. Plus, you need a new wardrobe. I threw out your stinky clothes, so all you have is the clothes you scrounged out of your backpack. And frankly, they don't look or smell very good either."

TM looked at her and frowned. "You are really bossy," he said. But his frown turned to a smile as he said, "But you're also pretty persuasive."

As they were being driven to San Jose, Cooper turned to TM and said, "I don't understand how Sage works."

"For the most part, hedge funds make a tremendous amount of money. Much of it is because they have the people to know where to invest and the resources to do large financial transactions. Sometimes they increase their returns by using leverage where the cost of borrowing is tiny compared to the expected returns. Some of the things they do are questionable, such as what's called front running, where they learn of a large pending trade by a third party and buy or sell in advance of the trade to take advantage of where the trade will take the market."

"I don't understand."

"Let's say they learn that a pension plan plans to sell a large block of a company's stock. The hedge fund will go in and sell the stock short. That means they sell the stock without owning it. When the large block hits the market, the price of the stock typically drops. So the hedge fund goes in and buys the stock at the lower price to cover its short position."

"How do they know the large block is about to be sold?"

"Because they're told about it by the large block seller's securities firm, whether it's an affiliate of the hedge fund or another securities fund. Hedge funds place a huge amount of trades through securities firms and pay millions of dollars of commissions even though they get special rates. The securities firms are eager to get the hedge funds' business so they give them tips from time to time, including about the trades some of their clients are making."

"But if a securities firm's client places a trade order, how is there time to alert the hedge fund?"

"The trade doesn't get placed until the securities firm initiates it, so there's plenty of time to alert the hedge fund. The hedge funds can place trades faster than most people can blink."

"But isn't that illegal?" Cooper asked.

"I don't know, but it's difficult to catch. What really crosses the line of legality is insider trading, where a firm places a trade based on confidential information obtained about what a company is going to do, such as make an acquisition. There can be a fine line here. In the industry, hedge funds and other firms that place trades are considered buyers, and the firms that compete to place the trades or provide other services are called sellers. The sellers are anxious to get business from the buyers and do everything they can to do so, ranging from exotic entertainment and expensive prostitutes to providing tips about specific stocks.

"Partly because of this, hedge funds typically have far more information about what's happening financially than anybody else. But what really crosses the line is when someone close to a company tips a hedge fund about some forthcoming event involving the company that will cause its stock to go higher or lower. These people are called tippors, and many times they're paid for providing the information."

"How do you know all this?" Cooper asked. "I know you're smart, but what I know of your background doesn't tell me you're some kind of financial expert. You're the dog man."

"Ouch. I'm not a financial expert, but I do my own investing and read business publications. But the main thing is what I learned from Natalie. We were together quite a bit and had time to talk, particularly when we rode horses from La Fortuna. She worked at Morgan's firm some summers and told me she learned a lot from Ken Alexander, the man who arranged the kidnapping and was murdered. She said he worked for a big investment firm on Wall Street, which is how he learned about *Sage*."

"How does *Sage* fit in to what you told me?"

"In recent years the government has really cracked down on insider trading. They monitor trading activity very closely and investigate if they see large trading volume just before some big corporate news is announced. When they have a suspicion about somebody, they'll go to court and get permission to tap the person's phone calls. When they find something, they work from the bottom up. They'll look for some lower-level person involved in the trading and try to get him to tell them who is involved. They'll look at e-mails and start to build a case. E-mail messages, text messages, and recorded phone calls have been the undoing of some big hedge fund managers.

"*Sage* is the answer to this. Instead of communicating by e-mail or phone, they use coded signals in the background of Internet videos. The videos may be on YouTube or even on a major news website. The signals are planted with such sophistication that anybody watching the video would have no idea that there is a secret message there. They also spread the trades so that there are several medium-size trades rather than a large trade that draws attention.

"They've been so successful that they've broadened their reach to increase the amount of inside information they obtain by bribing lawyers, accountants, corporate officials, and people in government. The volume now of inside trading is so great that the amount earned on each situation doesn't have to be so large. This makes detection all the more difficult."

"Wow. This certainly doesn't help the individual investor," Cooper said. "I just lowered my expectations of how much money I'll have in my IRA in the years ahead."

"There has always been insider trading, but there are two unique things about this. The first is how widespread and organized it is, with many firms apparently participating and many people being paid for tips. The second thing is the resort to violence. Insider trading is considered a white-collar crime. But these people are not hesitant to kill people who get in their way. This is as bad if not worse than what the mafia did some years ago."

"How much money do the people involved make?" Cooper asked.

"That's what so strange. A hedge fund manager who plays by the rules can make tens of millions a year, and you'd think that would be enough to satisfy anyone. But greed sets in, and they want more even though they live in high style. Many have fancy apartments in New York City as well as expensive vacation homes elsewhere and private jets. It's not unheard of for a hedge fund manager to hire a major entertainment facility for a night and have well-known entertainers there on the occasion of his birthday. Drug use certainly isn't unheard of."

"Would Morgan be in that crowd?"

"That's a good question. I've never met him, but what little I've learned about him seems to indicate that he lives more modestly. You wonder how he ever got involved."

"Hopefully we'll find out. When we get to San Jose we should call Barrett and Anderson and let them know I found you. They're anxious to hear. Also, this underscores the importance of keeping Morgan alive."

"So what do you have in mind for us to accomplish in San Jose?" TM asked.

"We'll meet with Chief Inspector Diaz and see if he has any ideas. It's a long drive from here to the United States, and the Pan-American Highway isn't the greatest road in the world."

"Well, since your drones can't take us, that leaves a boat or a plane."

"Do you have much money?" Cooper asked.

"Not on me, but there's still money from Morgan in my account in Boulder. Maybe Anderson can wire some to me in San Jose, but I don't want to have the same thing happen that happened after I got money in La Fortuna."

"Maybe you can have him wire the money to me?" Cooper asked.

"Can I trust you?" TM said with a frown.

"I don't know," Cooper said. "Maybe I could meet a cute Costa Rican and have a good time."

"He wouldn't be as good in bed as me."

"I'm still trying to find out how good you are. After all, we've only made love twice."

"I'll have to give you another demonstration tonight," TM said.

"What makes you think I'll let you?"

"I read your mind."

49

"Bad news," Cragin said. "The man got away, and a couple of people we had looking for him were killed."

"Do we have any idea where he is?" Bertre asked.

"The only thing we know for sure is that he's in Costa Rica. Our man who survived said a small helicopter dropped a bag full of black stuff that splattered the windshield of the car they were driving and the car went into a ditch and overturned."

"A helicopter? Good God. Who would have a helicopter and get involved?"

"I have no idea, and our man doesn't either. It's bizarre."

"That almost sounds like something the CIA would do, but why would they get involved? I stopped an effort by one of their people to investigate the situation, and I find it hard to believe they'd continue. I better check with my contact. He wasn't too happy when I asked him to intervene before. Do we have any way of tracking the man's location?"

"He doesn't seem to be using his cell phone. Our man is more determined than ever to find him, but it's not going to be easy."

"Well at least we know that at some point he'll try to get back to the States, and he has no idea what he'll find when he crosses the border and goes through immigration. We need to find him as soon as possible because we have another problem."

"What's that?"

"Morgan is getting worried that we might do something to him."

"I don't blame him," Cragin said. "I thought we should have taken him out already."

"As I told you, it's too risky. He's part of our circle, and other people in the circle could be upset if they found out we did something to him. In any event, he met with me and told me he had recorded a message revealing everything about Sage and put it in a safe deposit box to be opened if something happened to him."

"What did you say when he said that?" Cragin asked.

"I told him I was shocked. That he was part of our family and nothing happens to our family members."

"Was he satisfied?"

"He said that made him feel better, but he didn't say he would destroy the recording. I told him he was unnecessarily jeopardizing the rest of us and his own reputation. I told him that if he died from a heart attack or an accident, the recording could hurt a lot of people and be a big stain on his own reputation."

"Did that persuade him?"

"He said he'd think about it, but I doubt he'll change his mind."

"Now what do we do?"

"You were supposed to have a man keeping an eye on him. Do you?"

"Of course."

"Then he probably saw what bank Morgan went to."

"What if he did? Are we going to break into the bank?"

“Of course not. But there are a couple of possibilities. Neither one is very good.”

“Well, what are they?”

“We could send someone into Morgan’s house while he’s away and see if he can find the key to the safe deposit box. If he does, we can send someone to the bank posing as Morgan and retrieve what’s in the box.”

“What’s the other possibility?”

“We have someone accost Morgan and force him to go into the bank and get the recording.”

“But all he has to do is scream when he’s in the bank and we’re screwed.”

“I know. That’s why I said neither possibility is very good.”

“Is there anyone close to him that we can kidnap and threaten to kill if he doesn’t give us the recording?”

“Good question. We already killed his wife and his stepdaughter, but he may have kids of his own from his first marriage.”

“I’ll find out,” Cragin said.

Someone had been watching Morgan when he went to the bank to place the recording in the safe deposit box: one of Barrett’s detectives. But he did not know why Morgan went to the bank. The same detective had observed Morgan when he met with Bertre at the Wilmette lakefront park to tell him about the recording. And the detective had taken photographs of Bertre and had gotten the license number of the car that dropped him off and picked him up.

“We may be on to something,” Barrett said later when the detective reported what he had seen and showed Barrett the photographs. “People don’t usually have someone drive them to a park to talk to someone for a few minutes and then leave in the same vehicle. Did you trace the license number?"

"Yes. It's a black Lincoln MKS owned by a limo company. We'd like to find out who ordered the trip, but it's tricky. The limo company might tell its client if we made an inquiry."

"You were right not to make the inquiry. In the meantime, I'm getting pressure from the police chief, who in turn is getting pressure from the mayor. The mayor wants to know where things stand with the investigation. He's aware we're doing something because he sees the hours you and others are putting in, but he doesn't know what we're investigating. The chief and I don't want to tell him we're investigating Morgan because that would only lead to more questions, and you have to assume that anything you tell the mayor he will share with others. So I've been somewhat vague in what I tell him. I can keep doing that only so long. Cooper found TM, and they're on their way back to the States. He can't get here too soon."

50

Promptly at 9:00 a.m., Resto drove up to the front entrance of the Grand Hotel Costa Rica in San Jose to pick up TM and Cooper and take them to OIJ headquarters to meet Chief Inspector Diaz. They had enjoyed a leisurely breakfast at the hotel's ground-flood café, where they were able to relax and watch the people passing by. When they arrived at the building housing OIJ's headquarters, they were surprised to find it was unnecessary to pass through layers of security to get to the main office.

Diaz did not keep them waiting long. One of his assistants ushered them into Diaz's large office, which had rich, dark wood panels, a seating area, and a large mahogany desk.

With all of her conversations with Diaz held over the telephone, Cooper did not know what to expect when she saw him. With his powerful voice, she had expected to see a tall, heavyset person. But Diaz was a trim five foot seven with thick black hair that had streaks of gray at the temples. He rose from behind his desk to greet them.

"You must be Detective Cooper," he said as he shook her hand. "And this must be the mystery man with the tiny name that everybody wants to kill. Please be seated," he said as he led them to the seating area.

"We can't thank you enough for all you've done," Cooper said.

"I'm most grateful as well," TM said. "You probably saved my life."

"I am glad it worked out," Diaz said. "My men are still talking about your drones. I was hoping you'd leave them behind. But now the pressure is on me, and it's only a matter of time before we're going to have to get some drones ourselves."

Diaz paused and then said, "The men who were trying to kill you killed one of my police officers, and another was seriously wounded. The men were local mobsters. One of them survived but is still in critical condition, and we've been unable to find out who hired them. It's an extremely serious matter when one of our people is killed, let alone wounded, and we will not rest until we find the person or persons responsible. From everything I've heard, the ultimate responsibility rests with someone in the United States, and I am just as eager as you are to find the responsible people."

"That's great," TM said, "because we still need your help. The stepfather of the girl I rescued here is very much a key to finding the answers. I need to talk to him and convince him to tell us what he knows. There's a ring of powerful people in the securities industry who have discovered a way to hide their insider trading activities. They have tentacles throughout the business, financial, and even government sectors and are so powerful they were able to get me on a terrorist list, so I'll be taken into custody if I try to enter the country."

"Can you help us find a way to get him into the States without passing through immigration?" Cooper asked. "Time is of the essence."

There was silence.

"Have you heard the expression 'partnering with the devil'? We may have to do that, but we have to pick the right devil. It's no secret that a lot of drugs coming from Colombia go through Costa Rica on the Pan-American Highway. We try to interdict as much as we can and receive some financial and other assistance from the US to do that, but we probably miss most of it. We could intensify our efforts and put the squeeze on for a short while and try to get a major drug patron to arrange for TM to get across the border as a price for us backing off. But I don't want to deal with those people. The other alternative is coyotes. I'm sure that Detective Cooper, being from Arizona, is very familiar with coyotes."

"Of course," Cooper said.

"There are different levels of coyotes. At the bottom are the ones who promise desperate people everything and take all their money. They bring the people to the wall and help them climb over. Most of them are caught, and many of the rest wind up dead in the desert."

"I know," Cooper said. "It's awful."

"But at the top level, the coyotes have a high success rate. But it comes at a steep price."

"How are they so successful?" TM asked.

"Partly by bribing border patrol agents and partly by using false identification papers. I doubt either one would work with you, TM. But they have other ways they keep secret."

"How much do they charge?" TM asked.

"I'm not suggesting you pay anything."

"How do we accomplish it then?" Cooper asked.

"Leverage. We usually have some way to make life difficult for the drug or people traffickers even when we don't have enough information to charge them. The threat of this often gets us things from them that are not available otherwise. One of my good friends is a senior police official in Mexico City. I'll give him a call, and I'm sure he'll help us. I know how urgent this is from a time standpoint, so I suggest you book a flight to Mexico City. By the time you arrive, I'll have word from him about how you should proceed."

TM and Cooper looked at each other, and their expressions said the same thing. They had no choice.

"Let me know what flight you're on," Diaz said.

When they returned to their hotel, TM checked on the Internet and found a nonstop flight from San Jose to Mexico City at three p.m. on Aeromexico. He was able to book the last two seats.

They hurriedly checked out of the hotel and were driven to the airport by Resto. They each paid the departure tax of twenty-nine dollars with the equivalent amount of colones.

"This is crazy," Cooper said. "We're going to Mexico City, and we have no idea who we'll see, where we'll stay, or how long we'll be there. I don't think we'd do this for anyone other than Diaz."

"That's for sure. I'll call Diaz and tell him our flight number."

Before he crawled out of the overturned car, a dazed Professor groped Raiss's body until he found what he was looking for: the money he had given Raiss for the AK-47s. People were starting to gather around the car, and some wanted to help the Professor, whose face was puffed and whose clothes were stained with blood. But he pushed them away and made his way along the road until he finally accepted a ride from a man who stopped his car and offered to help. It was the man's last generous or other act, because he soon became a victim of the Professor's powerful grip around his neck.

The Professor drove the car a few miles until he found a side road where he could pull over and not be observed. He pulled the driver's body out of the car and dragged it several feet away from the road. The Professor's head throbbed and his body ached, so he spent the night in the car. The next day he drove to San Jose and found a market where he could park the car and use the men's room. He came out wearing the clothes of the man he had killed.

He slept the night in the car and woke up midmorning. He found a service station where he could wash his face and relieve himself, and then he drove to the San Jose International Airport, parked the car in the parking lot, and entered the terminal. He went straight to the ticket counter for United Airlines, where he booked a flight leaving that morning to Houston and connecting to another flight to Chicago. He had no luggage and made his way to the passenger gate area, where he waited in line and finally passed through security.

As he was headed to the gate for his flight, he looked back and hesitated. He saw a man standing in another line who looked vaguely familiar. The man was with a female companion. The Professor looked more closely, and it finally occurred to him who it might be. It was the man he had seen through the sight of his sniper rifle at Mata de Canan. It was TM.

The Professor turned and tried to get back to the area where he could see TM. But the security guards turned him away, and he soon saw TM and his companion board a plane and the door of the plane close behind them. The Professor strained to see the plaque with the flight number and destination. It was Aeromexico flight 657 to Mexico City. Thinking he had no realistic alternative, he boarded the United flight to Houston.

There were no two seats together on the flight to Mexico City. Cooper had a middle seat in aisle twenty-two of the 737 and TM had an aisle seat in the very last row. Unfortunately for him, it was next to the lavatory, and he had to endure people lined up for access as well as a not very pleasant aroma. The flight landed at eleven thirty a.m., nineteen minutes late.

There were only short lines for immigration, and they quickly reached the head of one of the lines and presented their passports. The immigration officer asked if they were married, and when Cooper said they were not, the officer motioned for TM to get back in line while he reviewed Cooper's passport. With a smile, he quickly handed it back to her, thanked her, and indicated she could pass through. TM stepped to the window and handed his passport to the officer, who swiped the front page through a scanner and then looked at a computer monitor. He frowned, peered intently at the monitor, and picked up a phone and began talking.

Could the United States immigration service have alerted Mexico to my presence on the list of terrorists? TM wondered. If so, he had a serious problem. Meanwhile, Cooper had passed through customs and exited to an area where people had gathered to meet arriving passengers. She turned, expecting to see TM, but he did not come out from customs. She started to walk back toward immigration but was stopped by an armed security guard who motioned for her to go back. Frustrated, she turned toward the waiting people. She was surprised to see a uniformed man holding a sign that read *COOPER*. She quickly walked up to the man and introduced herself.

"My name is Roberto Gonzalez," the man said. "I am an officer with the federal police. I'm here to escort you and a man to a meeting with my commander, Gualberte Perez."

"Thank you, Officer Gonzalez, but we have a problem. The man has not come through immigration. Can you take me back there so we can find out what is happening with him?"

"Of course," Gonzalez replied.

With that, he led Cooper back past the security guard to the station where TM was still standing.

"What's happening?" Gonzalez said to the immigration officer.

"We have a problem," the officer responded. "We recently started a program where we can screen passengers going to the United States using information from its Department of Homeland Security. This man's name, strange as it is, showed up as someone who is a person of interest to the department. We're required to notify the department when we encounter such a person."

"I don't understand," Gonzalez said. "This man just arrived in Mexico and is not on a flight to the United States. Why did you run the program?"

"Out of curiosity when I saw he was an American. I wanted to see how the program might work. Even though I didn't need to run the program for him, now that I did I must notify the US Department of Homeland Security."

"You do what you have to do," Gonzalez said, "but nothing says he's not entitled to enter Mexico, and he's coming with me."

"But I called my supervisor and he's on his way," the officer stammered. "Can't we wait for him?"

"No. We have been expecting this man. He has a meeting scheduled with my supervisor in the next few minutes, and we're late already."

With that, Gonzalez took TM's arm and motioned for him to proceed, and together with Cooper, they strode quickly through customs and left the departure area. Gonzalez led them out of the terminal to an unmarked black Chrysler sedan with tinted black windows parked in a prominently marked No Parking area. Gonzalez opened the rear passenger door and motioned TM to enter.

"Please sit in the front passenger seat," he said to Cooper as he opened the driver's side door and sat down.

A man in a neatly pressed uniform with two stars on the lapel sat in the back seat next to TM. He did not introduce himself.

"We have made a reservation for you on Aeromexico Flight seven-zero-six leaving today at three p.m. for Hermosillo," the man said to TM. "You will be met there by the people who will get you across the border."

"How?" TM asked.

"I didn't ask, and they wouldn't tell me if I did. Don't expect them to be very friendly. They are not doing this because they want to. You are fortunate that you worked with my friend Chief Inspector Diaz, because we would not do this just for anyone."

"How likely is it they will be successful in getting me across the border?" TM asked.

"Nothing is guaranteed," the man replied, "but they are very good at what they do, and they have a strong incentive to get you across safely without you being detained by your authorities."

"How will I know who they are and they know who I am?"

"You may not have known this, but one of Diaz's assistants photographed you and we sent a copy to them."

"Where will they cross the border?" Cooper asked. "Because I want to be there to meet him."

"They didn't tell me and I didn't ask. But if you look on a map, you will get some idea about the possibilities."

"I guess there's no point asking you when they'll take him across," Cooper said.

"You're right. You better get going, Mr. TM, because you have to purchase your ticket. One final word to both of you. This meeting never took place. Do you understand?"

"Yes," TM and Cooper replied in unison.

"There's a good chance they'll be taking you across at or near Nogales," Cooper said when they were back inside the terminal. "That's the closest border town to Hermosillo."

"I've never heard of Hermosillo," TM said.

"I've been to Hermosillo," Cooper said. "It's a large city and has several substantial businesses there, including manufacturing plants of US companies. There's no point in me flying with you to Hermosillo because I can't do much there. In fact, I might just be in the way."

"I agree," TM said. "Why don't you get a flight to Phoenix?"

"I will. Do you still have the cell phone you bought in Costa Rica?"

"No. One of the shops here may sell disposable cell phones. I'll buy one so I can call when I get past the border. I'll also call Anderson while we're here in the airport and let him know what's happening."

"Let's hope your friends let you keep your cell phone," Cooper said.

51

"Renzi's condition is good enough that we're bringing him here from the hospital for interrogation," Assistant Chief Inspector Munoz said to Diaz. "But I doubt he'll tell us much. He's one tough cookie. This is the only time I've wished our constitution didn't abolish the death penalty. We could have used that as a threat, but now he has no reason to talk."

"That remains to be seen," Diaz said. "Let me know when he's here."

When Diaz entered the interrogation room, Renzi was seated in a wheelchair next to a large steel table. Munoz and another inspector were seated to the left and right of Renzi. In accordance with standard practice, the session was being videotaped from an adjacent room that looked down on the interrogation room. The walls were stark white, and the ceiling had several spotlights that could be controlled by a remote in the hands of the other inspector.

Diaz sat down at the table opposite Renzi. By prearrangement, the three inspectors sat in silence and stared at Renzi.

Finally Renzi broke the silence. "You can stare all you want, but I have nothing to say to you."

The three inspectors continued to stare at Renzi in silence until Diaz slid a photo across the table in front of him. "This is the police officer you killed," Diaz said.

Renzi did not look down.

"Turn off the camera," Diaz ordered. "There's no worse crime than killing a police officer."

"I didn't kill this police officer or anyone else," Renzi defiantly said.

Diaz took the remote, pressed a button, and a panel on the wall slid up, revealing a large television screen. Diaz pressed another button, and a video appeared from the camera of the police vehicle where the shootout had taken place. It was somewhat grainy, but it showed two men firing weapons. One of them clearly was Renzi.

"I've got nothing to say."

"I'm sure you'll be sent to jail for life for killing a police officer. It's another question how long that life will be."

"What do you mean?" Renzi shouted.

"After you're convicted, we'll take you to the federal prison where you'll be in the company of some not very nice people. You better hope they like you."

"Why?" Renzi asked.

"The last person they didn't like was found mysteriously dead in his cell. Of course we wouldn't tell them things that might cause them to dislike you."

"This is outrageous!" Renzi shouted. "You have no right to do this."

"We won't be doing anything except following the letter of the law," Diaz said softly. "The rest will simply be nature taking its course."

"But you'll be encouraging the prisoners to take my life."

"We would be doing no such thing. We would only be letting them know some things about you, including a rumor that you are a pedophile. As bad as prisoners may be, they hate pedophiles."

"I'm not a pedophile," Renzi shouted.

"I didn't say you were. Only that there was a rumor that you are."

There was silence again for several minutes. Diaz pressed a button on the remote that restarted the video cameras.

Renzi finally broke the silence. "What do you want to know?"

"We want to know who contacted you to have people killed," Diaz said forcefully.

There was silence again.

"What would happen if, hypothetically, I told you?"

"It depends. If the information we get enables us to locate the person who initiated the contact and we are able to bring him here for a trial, it would make a huge difference. The person who gave us the information probably would not be sent to the federal prison."

"His name is Alfred Cragin."

"How did he contact you?"

"He flew here in a private jet and called me from the airport."

"How did he know to call you?"

"He didn't say, and I didn't ask him."

"What did he say he wanted?"

"To hire men who were willing and able to eliminate his enemies."

"Did he say who the enemies were?"

"No."

"You're lying."

"No, no, I'm not lying."

"We can end this now as far as I'm concerned," Diaz said and got up and walked toward the door.

"Wait. He told me there were two people who were his enemies at a company called Rand Trading Company. One of them had kidnapped the daughter of one of his friends, and he wanted him to be questioned about the kidnapping."

"And?"

"My men found out that the kidnapping had been faked and the daughter was part of the scheme."

"Were you there?"

"No."

"What happened next?"

"I called Cragin and reported this to him, and he said we had to find the daughter and eliminate her. You know the rest."

"How much did he pay you?"

"Ten thousand dollars."

"Did he wire it to you?"

"No. He gave it to me in cash when he was here with the plane."

"We want the phone number you called and the exact date and time he was here on the plane."

"OK," a somber Renzi said. "I will get that for you."

52

Cooper and TM briefly hugged before he headed for the departure gate.

"Good luck," she said. "I'll be on pins and needles waiting to hear from you."

"Thanks for all you've done for me," TM said. "I'll get across one way or another."

His seat was better on this flight. He had an aisle seat in the fifteenth row of the 737. It was a smooth flight with a smooth landing, and the plane quickly taxied to its arrival gate. He walked through a concourse to the main terminal area, all the while looking for someone to meet him. It was not until he was about to leave the terminal that a man stepped next to him.

"Keep walking, gringo," the man said.

They exited the terminal, and the man guided TM along a sidewalk into a covered parking area and to a 2005 green Ford Taurus where he stopped. He turned TM and thoroughly searched his body. He removed TM's cell phone, opened the right rear passenger door, and motioned to TM to get in, which TM did. There was a man sitting in the rear seat opposite TM and a man in the driver's seat. The man who had met TM in the terminal took the seat next to the driver. Wordlessly the driver started the motor, and they drove away.

It took them several minutes to get through the heavy truck traffic in the city, but they finally came to the outskirts and to a two-lane road headed north. The men in the car did not say one word to TM or to each other, and he did not say one word to them. They had driven for about two hours when the driver pulled the car to the side of the road and stopped. The man next to TM placed a hood over his head that prevented him from seeing anything but allowed him to breathe comfortably. The man then bound TM's hands together at the wrists with a leather strap. Again, not one word was spoken.

The Mexican official had said they would not be very friendly, TM recalled, but he hadn't expected them to be like this. He hoped the Mexican Federal Police officer was being truthful when he said the men had a strong incentive to get him across the border. The one thing that gave TM comfort was Diaz. He had been so open and helpful that TM felt he would not have set something up that was not authentic.

They drove several more minutes until the car came to a stop. The car door next to him opened, and a hand reached in and brought him to his feet. The person then guided TM forward until TM's foot stubbed something. Slowly he lifted his right foot forward and came down on a step. He then alternated stepping up a staircase until he reached the top and was able to walk slowly forward. The person then pushed TM's chest, and TM sat back on what he thought was a bench or a chair. He was left sitting there for what seemed to be an eternity.

Finally someone came and pulled him to his feet and walked him forward until he came to what seemed like a platform that swayed slightly from side to side. His escort gently but firmly grasped his arm and the platform began to descend. TM had no idea how far it dropped until it finally stopped. He was then led forward on an uneven surface. A couple of times he stumbled and almost fell, but his escort kept him upright. He continued to walk for several feet until the person had him lift his feet slightly and step onto something more firm.

The grip on TM's arm tightened slightly as the platform began to rise. It rose slowly for a few minutes until it stopped, and he was led forward onto a hard surface. He walked slowly until he was stopped, and he heard a car door opening. He was pushed gently into the back seat of what seemed to be a car. He heard the front two car doors open and then close. He could hear the sound of a garage door being opened, and soon he felt the vehicle drive forward.

He could not tell how far the car had driven, but he knew it had been moving for at least fifteen minutes before it came to a stop. The passenger door next to him opened, and the leather straps that had been binding his wrists together were removed. He was pulled from the vehicle while at the same time the hood was removed from his head.

He was blinded for a few moments by the light, but then he turned to see the person who had been guiding him. He was stunned to see that she was one of the most beautiful women he had ever seen. She was Mexican, with shoulder-length black hair, dark brown eyes, and gorgeous features. The dark blue top and matching pants she wore could not conceal her beautiful figure.

"Good luck, sir," the woman said as she handed him his cell phone. "You are at the bus stop, and here is your ticket to Tucson."

Before he could say anything, she was back in the car, and it drove away. TM looked around and could see that he was on the

US side of the border approximately one hundred yards from the entrance gates. To his right was a bus stop, and a bus with the letters TUFESA was parked there. He walked to the door of the bus, handed his ticket to the driver, and took one of the few empty seats.

He thought back to what Inspector Diaz had said about leverage. Whatever leverage the Mexican police had on the people who had brought him across the border must have been huge. He tried to call Cooper, but there was no answer. He left a voice mail that he was on a bus headed for Tucson and would call her when he was there. He then called Anderson.

"I made it," TM said when Anderson answered. "I'm on a bus to Tucson."

"Great," Anderson said. "You can catch a plane there and fly to Denver."

"I'm afraid not. I'm probably still on the watch list. I'll probably have to rent a car unless Cooper has a different idea."

53

"We located one of Morgan's kids," Cragin said. "Her name is Susan Waters. She's married and has a young daughter."

"Where does she live?" Bertre asked.

"In La Grange, a suburb of Chicago. Should we grab her?"

"No," Bertre exclaimed. "That would be a big mistake. It's better to let Morgan know that we know where his daughter lives and she can come to harm if he doesn't give us the recording."

"I understand. We've also learned that the TM man was in Mexico City. We heard this from our man and also from our contact at Homeland Security who said they were told by the security people at the Mexico City airport."

"That's not really surprising. He'll get the real surprise when he tries to enter the country."

"How do we let Morgan know we'll harm his daughter if he doesn't give us the recording?" Cragin asked.

"Good question," Bertre said. "It shouldn't be me, and he doesn't know you."

"I have a suggestion you may not like."

"Let's not play games; spit it out."

“Let’s use the man who was working for us in Costa Rica and is now on the way back. He’s called the Professor because he’s so smart.”

“Well, he wasn’t smart enough to catch the TM person and eliminate him.”

“He came close. He was in Special Forces in the army and is trained to do just about everything. He could certainly get Morgan’s attention.”

Bertre was silent for a few moments. “I don’t have a better idea,” he finally said.

“One more thing,” Cragin said. “I know you’ve resisted this, but once the Professor gets the recording, he needs to eliminate Morgan.”

“Under the circumstances,” Bertre said. “I can’t argue with you.”

TM was able to transfer to another bus in Tucson that took him to Phoenix. He took a cab to the Biltmore area, where he bought some new clothes and also went to the Apple store and purchased a new iPhone. He made sure he got a new number and a different provider, AT&T. Cooper didn’t answer when he called her, but he left a voice mail giving her his number. His phone rang almost immediately.

“I didn’t recognize the number,” she said. “Where are you?”

“I’m in Phoenix.”

“Terrific. I’m in my office. Can you come over here?”

“Be right there.”

“My you look smart,” Cooper said when she saw him. “It’s amazing what new clothes can do. How did you get across the border?”

"It was an unbelievable experience. The people who got me across didn't say one word until the very end when one of them wished me good luck."

He intentionally did not describe that person.

"I had a hood over my head," he continued, "but I'm quite sure I went through a tunnel. They were careful not to let me see either the place where it started or the place where it ended. They drove me to a bus stop and even gave me a ticket to Tucson."

"They did good," Cooper said. "It's great to see you."

"Let's get Anderson and Barrett on the phone and talk about what happens next," TM said.

Anderson and Barrett were both available, and TM brought them up to date about what had happened with him.

"Is there anything new at your place?" TM asked Barrett.

"We're still trying to keep an eye on Morgan, but except for one meeting he had at a lakefront park, he hasn't done anything unusual or had any unusual visitors. He was met at the park by a man who was driven there and back in a sedan. The sedan is licensed to a limousine company, and we didn't think it wise to inquire who hired the company. What's our plan?"

"Unfortunately, I'll be driving rather than flying to your place because I may be on the watch list. Cooper will be with me, so we'll drive straight through, which means we should get there in about two days. Once we do, I plan to visit Mr. Morgan. Let's hope I can persuade him to give himself up and expose the ring."

"The mayor said several members of the city council are beginning to think we're incompetent," Evanston's police chief said to Sergeant Barrett. "He's given us a one-week deadline. Unless we have something positive to report by then, 'heads will roll,' to use his words."

"What does that mean?" Barrett asked.

"He didn't say, but to cover my ass, I told him that if we don't have something in a week, I'll assign someone else to the case to replace you. Will you have something by then?"

"A man is coming here in the next couple of days, and hopefully we'll know one way or another then."

54

Jeffrey Morgan was distraught. All kinds of things were going through his mind. He was not sure he had done the right thing telling Bertre that he had made a recording about Sage. He'd probably taken it as a sign of lack of trust and maybe even defiance. It was crystal clear that Bertre would stop at nothing to protect the ring. Maybe he would even blow up the bank where Morgan had the safe deposit box if he knew which one it was. So he didn't feel completely safe with the hidden recording. It might not be as strong a defense as he had thought.

He had left a sealed envelope with his estate-planning attorney that was only to be opened at his death. But a recording of a dead man was not as powerful as a live witness. On the other hand, he wouldn't feel safe going to the FBI or some other government agency. The ring's tentacles extended throughout the government, and being an informer would seal his fate.

He felt responsible for the deaths of his lawyer and friend Webster, his wife, and now his stepdaughter. *I'm actually a murderer*, he thought to himself. Maybe the only honorable thing for him to do was to take his own life. He decided he needed to get away and think about his situation.

He went upstairs to the master bedroom and to a small safe in the corner of the master closet. He hadn't used the safe for some time and wasn't sure if he remembered the combination. His first try didn't work. Neither did his second. *I've got to relax,* he said to himself. He waited a few moments and then tried again. This time it opened.

He reached inside and took out a Ruger .38 pistol. It wasn't loaded, but there was a box of bullets in the bottom drawer of the nightstand on his side of the bed. He retrieved the box and put the pistol and the box in a small cloth bag he found in the closet.

He needed to go somewhere, but where would he go? He didn't like the idea of going somewhere and sitting in a hotel room. Then he thought of a place. A few years ago he had purchased an A-frame in a subdivision that had private lake rights at Lake Geneva, Wisconsin. He had purchased it for his children and their spouses and kids and had the title taken by a trust for the benefit of his children from his first wife. He had spent very little time there and didn't even have a key. But he thought his children left a key under a mat next to the front door.

This being a Monday, he was sure none of his children were there since they had jobs to go to. He packed some of his clothes in a suitcase and loaded the suitcase, the cloth bag with the gun, and a few other items into his Lexus LS460 sedan in his enclosed garage. He took his cell phone but didn't plan to tell anyone where he was going.

He opened the garage door and drove out, closing the door behind him. He drove to Lake Street and then to the Edens Expressway, where he took a spur to Highway 294 headed for Wisconsin. As he was driving, he tried to think where things had gone wrong. His father had been a vice-president of the First

National Bank of Chicago. Things were different then. Banks took deposits and made loans while investment banks such as Goldman Sachs managed public and private securities offerings and also acted as merger and acquisition advisors. As the years passed and government regulations were relaxed, banks moved into investment banking, and hedge funds began to proliferate.

When Morgan graduated from Harvard Business School, he was offered jobs by several investment banks and hedge funds. He took a job in New York City as a bond trader with an investment bank. As time went on, he moved into trading stocks and new, sophisticated products such as derivatives. It was heady stuff, and his income increased substantially. He was recruited by a medium-sized hedge fund headed by Bertre, where he learned new ways of generating profits. The firm grew substantially, partly, he found, because it was able to trade stocks in advance of significant news about companies. It was able to buy calls on a stock just hours before the company made an announcement that caused the stock price to increase well above the call price.

He soon learned that this was not due to good fortune or good research. It was due to someone with advance knowledge of the announcement tipping someone at the firm where he worked about what would be announced. That was the time, he now thought, when he should have disengaged. But the money was too good. He had an expensive apartment near his office on Wall Street and enjoyed an active social life. He fell in love with a woman who worked at a major securities firm, and they were married in an elaborate ceremony that took place on a cruise ship in the Caribbean with several invited guests.

They had two children who were still young when Morgan discovered that his wife was having an affair with one of his friends. He was devastated. Thanks to an expensive attorney and an expensive settlement, he was able to get a divorce and sole custody of the children. He had decided then to move back to the Chicago area, where he would feel more comfortable raising his children. He married again, this time to a woman who worked as an administrator at a hospital and was everything he could have hoped for in a wife. He started his own investment firm with the financial help of Bertre, who invested several million dollars in the fund.

It wasn't until the last few years that Bertre had brought Morgan into the ring with Sage. He should have known better than to get involved with Sage, but he had felt obligated to Bertre partly because Bertre's returns from the money he had invested in Morgan's fund were mediocre.

It was almost dark when he arrived at the A-frame. Sure enough, there was a key under the mat. *Probably the first place a burglar would look,* he thought to himself.

He took his things inside and checked the kitchen to see what was available for him to eat and drink. He found nothing to eat but plenty of beer to drink. He settled into a comfortable chair in the living room and felt somewhat better already. He figured he had four days without any of his children showing up. That would give him time to think about what he should do and whether he should take his own life. He took the Ruger and the box of bullets out of the cloth bag and inserted six bullets into the chambers. One thing was clear to him: if he decided to take his own life, he would go somewhere else in the area rather than tarnish the place his children loved so much.

55

TM and Cooper set out for Illinois in Cooper's 2012 Ford Edge SUV. They drove through Payson, Arizona, and along state highways until they were able to drive onto I-40 headed east. They had folded down the rear seats of the Edge so one of them could partially stretch out while the other drove. But most of the time they were seated together in the front. They mostly rode in silence but found things to talk about from time to time.

"What are you going to say to Morgan?" Cooper asked.

"The first thing I'll do is tell him in graphic detail everything that happened, including the death of his stepdaughter. I'll tell him that she told me about Sage and his involvement in the ring and try to persuade him to expose Sage."

"What if he refuses?"

"I'll tell him he's a dead man walking because of the brutality of the ring and that the only chance he has to live is to cooperate with the authorities."

Cooper drove the first segment of their trip and bragged to TM about the great mileage her Edge was getting. They finally stopped near Albuquerque for fuel and lunch. When they resumed the trip, TM took over as the driver.

"Were you born and raised in Arizona?" TM asked.

"Yes," Cooper replied. "One of the few. I was raised in Phoenix and went to a Phoenix public elementary school and a public high school. My father was a plumber and never finished high school. He was bound and determined for me and my brother to go to college."

"Is your brother older or younger than you?"

"Older, but he was killed in Iraq. That happened a little more than a year ago. It was an IED."

"I'm very sorry. I'll bet you were very popular when you were in school."

"No. I was not one of the popular kids. I was too busy studying so I could make my father proud."

"What about when you went to college? Were you in a sorority?"

"No. The University of Arizona is very Greek oriented, but I decided not to pledge. I did have boyfriends, but my social life was rather restrained."

"Does that mean boring?"

"Hardly. But I didn't attend any of the drunken parties."

"When I first saw you, you wore clothes that understated your attractiveness."

"That was intentional. When I went to work for DPS, I found it wasn't wise to appear in any way sexy, either within the organization or with outsiders."

"Even when you weren't working?"

"Of course not. I'm a woman, and in my private life I did want to be attractive to men. But I certainly didn't want to look like a sexpot. We've talked enough about me. Anderson told me you were married and your wife was killed. Would you mind if I asked you what happened?"

There was silence for a few moments.

"She was an agent with the Drug Enforcement Agency, and I worked for them as an outside contractor. We were sent undercover to Colombia to find a drug lord high on the list of DEA's most wanted."

"Did you find him?"

"Yes, through his obsession to have the best show horses."

"Was she killed in Colombia?"

"No. We weren't married when we were in Colombia. In fact, we didn't really like each other when we first met. But we went through a lot and got married when we got back to the States."

"Was she killed in an accident?"

"No. She was shot. The drug lord sent his enforcer to the United States to assassinate the people who would testify against him. The enforcer was able to kill a person in the witness protection program and another who had armed marshals guarding him. The enforcer used a sniper gun to kill my wife while she was riding a horse not far from my place in Colorado."

"Were you able to catch the enforcer?"

"I was on a horse several yards away trying to catch up with her to tell her she was in danger when I saw her get hit and fall off her horse. I went after the enforcer and killed him, but my wife couldn't be saved."

"How horrible," Cooper said softly.

They drove on in silence and changed drivers from time to time.

"It was good of your boss to let you drive with me to Illinois," TM said as they were pulling away from a service station near St. Louis, Missouri.

"As a matter of fact, he wasn't too happy about it. He said that now that you're back in the States, he didn't see any way to justify

Arizona being involved. He thought the state's involvement in this matter was tenuous before and now it's even worse. He expects me back within a week. Are you glad I came?"

"Of course. I never could have made it this fast driving by myself."

"Oh," an obviously disappointed Cooper said softly.

"But it's much more than that," TM said, realizing he had made a mistake. "I love to be with you."

"You're just saying that."

"No. No. It's true."

They were driving a few miles north of Springfield, Illinois, when TM suddenly said, "I should have thought about this sooner."

"What are you talking about?" Cooper asked.

"The gold certificate. I delivered a gold certificate to Ulate. We know he and Natalie's friend Kenneth were killed, but we don't know what happened to the gold certificate. In all likelihood, the murderers took it, but Webster told me there were only a few places where the certificate could be converted into a recognized currency."

"The people involved with Sage certainly would know how to do that," Cooper said.

"Yes they would. But that assumes the murderers were kind enough to deliver the certificate to the *Sage* people."

"We'll probably never know."

56

When TM and Cooper arrived in Evanston, they checked into the Hilton Garden Inn in the downtown area. After they had showered and changed into fresh clothes, they drove the short distance to Evanston Police Headquarters, where they asked for Sergeant Barrett.

"I know Inspector Cooper," Barrett said, "so you must be the infamous TM. It's a relief to see you, but I don't have good news. We don't know where Morgan is. Our man who was watching him saw him drive away from his home a few days ago to a major expressway and head north. Once he crossed the state line into Wisconsin, our man stopped following him, so we think he's in Wisconsin but we don't know where."

"Great," TM said. "So let's find him. The people who were after Natalie and me in Costa Rica seemed to be able to trace my location by my cell phone signal. Surely if they were able to do that in Costa Rica, we should be able to trace Morgan's location that way here."

"Things may be easier in Costa Rica. Assuming he had his cell phone with him and it was turned on, we should be able to trace him in Illinois because of our relationship with the cell phone providers. But that won't do us much good unless he comes back to Illinois. We need the assistance of the police in Wisconsin."

"How do we get that?" Cooper asked.

"I'm thinking," Barrett replied. "The FBI could get it for us, but we can't take a chance and contact them because we don't know if people there are involved with Sage."

"Do we even know his cell phone number?" TM asked.

"Fortunately we do," Barrett replied.

"What have we got to lose?" Cooper said. "Why don't you just ask a police department there?"

"What reason do I give?" Barrett asked.

"Given what we know, and I certainly know it well," TM said, "Morgan is, at the very least, a suspected accomplice in multiple homicides."

"I'll see what I can do," Barrett said.

"We have some information about Cragin," Assistant Chief Inspector Hector Munoz reported to Diaz. "Fortunately the private plane that brought him to San Jose to meet with Renzi filed a manifest with his name and address on it. He lives in New York City in an apartment on Park Avenue, which means he's very wealthy. He seems to be self-employed. He does not have a criminal record."

"Do we have anything else that would place him in San Jose when Renzi said they met?" Chief Inspector Diaz asked.

"We do. Renzi gave us a detailed description of Cragin and we found two people at the private airplane facility who remember him."

"That's good enough for me," Diaz said. "Let's file charges against him and prepare extradition papers."

"It worked," Barrett said. "The Kenosha County Sheriff's Department agreed to help us. We should be hearing from them soon. But I have a problem."

"What's that?" TM asked.

"My police chief gave me a week to come up with a major development in the Webster murder or he'll take me off the case and assign someone else. The week is up tomorrow."

"Isn't TM being here a major development?" Cooper asked. "Let TM talk to the chief."

"I already talked to the chief about TM, but he said that TM can't solve the case. He was in Costa Rica when Webster was killed, and everything he knows about Morgan's involvement is hearsay. Besides, there's nothing that can be announced publicly."

"Who would take your place?" TM asked.

"Probably Corporal Winston. He's very methodical and probably would take a week or two to review our case file before he would make a decision about anything."

"Great," Cooper said. "Too bad Chief Inspector Diaz isn't in the United States."

"Speaking of Diaz," TM said, "would it help if he talked to your chief? He certainly knows things that are real and not hearsay. Like dead bodies."

"That's a good thought," Barrett said. "Let's go talk to him."

Diaz was very persuasive. He explained in great detail the murders that had taken place and the attempts on the lives of TM and Natalie, which ultimately resulted in her death.

"I know you're only investigating the murder of a lawyer who lived in your town. But he is one of a number of dots that are connected, and I think it's urgent to pursue this further. One of my officers was killed, and we are actively pursuing leads on our end."

"He's right," Barrett said after the call ended. "Webster was Morgan's lawyer, Natalie was Morgan's stepdaughter, and TM was hired by Morgan. And then there's the unexpected suicide of Morgan's wife."

The police chief was silent for a few moments. "You're right," he finally said. "I'm going to have to tell the mayor that we have a major investigation underway and we can't talk about the details or it could compromise the investigation. He's going to press me for details and timing and I'll just have to be seemingly forthcoming yet nonspecific."

The report from the Kenosha County Sheriff's Department was of limited help. They were able to determine that Morgan had been in Kenosha County and had driven west into Walworth County, but the cell phone signal ended shortly after he entered that county.

"It's hard to believe he was driving aimlessly," Cooper said. "He must have had some destination in mind."

"A lot of people here have second homes in Wisconsin, and he may have one too," Barrett said. "We'll call the county clerk's office in Walworth County and see if they have a record of any property owned by Morgan."

The clerk's office responded promptly. The answer was negative.

"Natalie told me Morgan had two daughters by his first wife," TM said. "If we can contact one of them, she might be able to help us. We really can't ask Morgan's secretary, but there's another possibility. Webster was more than a lawyer for Morgan. He was also a friend. Roger, can you ask Webster's wife what she knows about Morgan's children?"

"Good idea," Barrett said. "I'll call her."

A few minutes later he reported that Morgan had a daughter named Susan Waters living in La Grange, Illinois.

"We checked the phone company records and found a Thomas Waters, the only Waters we found in La Grange," Barrett said. "We have the address and phone number. The tricky part is how we approach Susan Waters."

TM and Barrett both looked at Cooper.

Cooper easily found the address of Thomas Waters. It was in an old but well-maintained neighborhood with large two- and three-story homes with large front lawns. The Waters's residence had a white stucco exterior and a large screened-in front porch. Cooper could see it would not be easy to observe comings and goings at the Waters residence because all the homes had driveways, and there were no cars parked on the street. She parked the Edge in the parking lot of a train station two blocks away and took out her laptop. She went to Facebook and using some methods taught her by an old hand at DPS, found that Susan Waters was a big user of the social media site. As she went through the many postings, she saw several photos of Waters and came across a posting that made her sit up.

There was a photo of a Waters and a young girl sitting on chairs on what looked like the porch of a small A-frame house. The caption read:

Cissy and me at our lake house on a beautiful day at Lake Geneva.

Cooper immediately called TM.

"I'm reasonably sure the daughter and her husband have a lake house at a lake called Geneva," she said. "But now the question becomes exactly where."

"I'll ask Barrett to help me find where Lake Geneva is, and then I'll rent a car and drive up to the area," TM said. "In the meantime, I'll ask Barrett to check with the Walworth County Clerk to see if there's a property listed under the name Thomas Waters."

As Cooper was thinking about how she could get the opportunity to talk to Susan Waters, a commuter train pulled into the station. As Cooper watched people step to the platform from the two-level train, she was startled to see a woman whose face looked familiar. It was Susan Waters. She was dressed in a dark gray two-piece pantsuit with a crisp white shirt that cried out she was a professional woman.

Cooper quickly got out of the Edge and came abreast of Waters. She turned to her and said, "Excuse me, but I think I know you from somewhere."

Waters turned and gave Cooper a hard look.

"You don't look familiar," Waters said.

"Maybe I'm mistaken, but I thought I met you at Lake Geneva. My husband and I have been looking at possibly buying a place there, and our real estate agent introduced us to a number of people."

"We have a place at Lake Geneva, but I don't remember meeting you," Waters said.

"Well, maybe you can give me some idea about the best place to buy," Cooper said.

"Our place is located in a subdivision called Lakeside. We're not on the lake, but we have lake rights and a buoy for our boat. Have you looked at properties there?"

"No, we haven't. Where on the lake is it located?"

"It's on the west side of the lake in Fontana. I'm surprised your real estate agent hasn't taken you there."

"Maybe we need a new agent," Cooper said. "We'll have to look at Lakeside. I have to run, but maybe we'll see each other there."

A puzzled look came on Waters's face. "What's your name?" she asked.

"Carson Cooper," Cooper answered and quickly walked away.

"It's in a subdivision called Lakeside," Cooper said on the phone to TM. "It's in Fontana. Maybe it's in Susan's name rather than her father's or husband's."

"I'll have Barrett check. In the meantime, I'll look for Lakeside and see if I can drive around in it. I hope it's not a gated community."

During the call with Barrett, TM found out that Morgan had been driving a Lexus sedan. The Lakeside subdivision was not a gated community, and TM was easily able to drive through an entrance gate. The streets in the subdivision wound around several small hills, and the homes were built on a hill rising above the lake. They were pleasant but modest and stood very close to each other. Most of them did not have garages. It was apparent that most of the properties were second homes because there was no sign of people.

As TM turned down one of the narrow streets, he was startled to see a Lexus sedan in the driveway of one of the homes, a wooden A-frame. He noted the address and texted it to Cooper. Taking a chance, he parked his car in one of the neighbor's driveways and walked to the A-frame, where he walked up a few steps to a deck and pressed the doorbell.

Morgan was startled. *Who could that possibly be?* His first inclination was to ignore the doorbell, but that could lead to more trouble. He went to the cloth bag, removed the Ruger .38, and held it behind him as he walked to the door. It was made almost entirely of glass, and he could see a man standing in front of it. His hand with the Ruger shook, but he kept it behind him. Before he could say anything, the man spoke up.

"I'm TM," the man said. "The person you hired to find your daughter. I'd like to talk to you."

A look of terror crossed Morgan's face. He had never seen TM and had no idea what he looked like. Could this be someone who was sent by Bertre to kill him?

"You hired me to go with my dogs to Flagstaff to see if your daughter was one of the victims of a serial killer. Your attorney Webster then hired me on your behalf to go to Costa Rica to rescue her from a kidnapper. I did, but as you know, we were hunted down and she was killed. Let me in so we can deal with a bad situation for both of us. I assure you, I won't harm you."

TM lifted his arms and said, "I am not armed."

Morgan was stunned. The man knew too much to be someone sent to kill him. If this man really was TM, he should believe he wouldn't harm him. But why was he here? Morgan decided to open the door but kept the Ruger behind him. He motioned for TM to sit on a couch in the living room while he took a seat behind a small table in the corner of the room.

"Why are you here?" Morgan asked.

"I told you. This is a bad situation for both of us. Several attempts have been made to kill me, and you could be next. I know Webster was killed, and I was devastated when they also killed Natalie. They desperately want to kill me because they correctly suspect I know about Sage."

Morgan swung his arm around and pointed the Ruger at TM. "If I kill you now, maybe all my problems can go away."

TM stood up and spread his arms. "Go ahead."

Morgan's hands shook, and after a few moments he put the Ruger on the table. "I couldn't shoot you."

"I know," TM said.

"What should I do?" Morgan asked.

"We have to expose Sage. I know doing that would incriminate you. But if we do it right, we'll get you in a position where you'll get a minimal sentence and very possibly no jail time."

"I've been thinking about this, and maybe the best thing I can do is take my own life."

"You have two daughters and a granddaughter. Do you really want to hurt them?"

"Maybe they'd rather have me dead than be exposed as a criminal."

"You're wrong. Totally wrong. You're their father and grandfather. They would stick with you and be supportive. The worst thing you could do is shame them by committing suicide."

They sat in silence for several moments.

"You're right. But you don't realize the tremendous hold the Sage ring has on people in all government agencies. We can't rely on any government people to help us."

"Even the FBI?"

"Even the FBI. Maybe it's hopeless."

"No, it's not. I think I have a way. Let's stay here tonight and drive back in the morning. It's best if you give me the handgun."

Morgan looked at it for a few moments and then handed it to TM.

57

The next morning TM and Morgan drove to Morgan's home. When they arrived, Morgan used the garage door opener in his car to open the garage door and drove inside. TM parked his car in the driveway, and he and Morgan entered the house through a door in the garage. Morgan led the way through the kitchen and dining room but stopped when he came to the living room. He was stunned. A man was sitting in a living room chair holding a Glock that was pointed at Morgan.

"What are you doing here!" Morgan shouted as TM halted beside him.

"I was sent here to see you, but what a pleasant surprise," the Professor said. "You brought with you the one person I most wanted to find. Put your hands out to the side, and don't make a wrong move."

"This is the man who killed Natalie," TM said.

"And you're the one who killed one of my friends and was responsible for the death of the other. For this you will die. And as for you, Mr. Morgan, we want the recording you made and put in a safe deposit box. We're holding your daughter in La Grange and will kill her unless you give me the recording."

"Two days ago I was ready to take my own life," Morgan said. "But now I'm going to do what's right. I hold the high card. If I'm dead, or if anything happens to my daughter, the recording will be released and the whole house will come tumbling down."

The Professor jumped up from his chair, aiming his first shot at TM. But TM had stepped to his right and quickly fired two bullets from the Ruger. The first hit the Professor in his right shoulder and the second in his right leg. The Professor gasped and tried to turn to fire, but Morgan ran forward and wrestled the Glock out of his hand and onto the floor. TM picked it up with his left hand and handed it to Morgan.

"Sit down," TM shouted at the Professor, "or the next bullet will find your heart."

TM had Morgan take off his belt and use it to bind the Professor's wrists together behind his back. TM called Barrett, and within minutes two Evanston police cars and an emergency vehicle were in front of the house. A Kenilworth police car appeared soon after.

The emergency medical technicians tended to the Professor's wounds and stopped the bleeding. He was then put on a stretcher and taken to Evanston Hospital with two Evanston police officers riding with him. TM and Morgan got into TM's rental car and drove to the Evanston Police Department headquarters, where Cooper was waiting.

58

Morgan was relieved to hear no harm had come to his daughter. He was read his rights and asked if he wanted a lawyer. He declined. He was taken to an interview room where, with a video recorder running, he described the workings of the Sage ring and identified Bertre as the leader. He said that Bertre had ordered the murder of Webster and Natalie. He said they had even murdered his wife and made it look like suicide.

"Where do we go from here?" Barrett asked. "We need to get a federal law enforcement agency involved, but how do we do that when we don't know who we can trust? It's incredible that they were even able to get TM on the highest terrorist list."

"I know some people I trust in the US Attorney's Office in Phoenix, but you can't count on them without knowing what their superiors will do," Cooper said.

"We need to do something that will make it impossible for this to be ignored," TM said. "Do you have an office where I can make a private call?"

Barrett found an open office for TM and closed the door behind him. TM placed a call to the office of Susan Ward, the assistant administrator of the Special Operations Division of the Drug Enforcement Administration.

"Susan Ward's office," a voice announced.

"This is TM."

"Of course. One moment, please."

"What are you up to?" Susan said. "Are you ready to come back to work for us? By the way, I miss you."

"I've had my hands full, Susan. After I get some rest maybe I can come back. But right now, I need a favor."

"What's that?"

TM told her what he wanted.

The next day Mitchell Vargas drove up and parked his car in the Evanston Police Department parking lot. As he walked to the door, he was surprised to see Stephen Fishman.

"What are you doing here?" Vargas asked Fishman.

"I got a tip from an anonymous source," Fishman answered.

"Anonymous my foot," Vargas said. "I'll bet it's the same as mine."

They entered the building together and after clearing security, were escorted to a conference room. Waiting for them were Evanston's mayor, the police chief, Sergeant Barrett, Morgan, Cooper, and TM.

Vargas was one of the top financial reporters for the *Wall Street Journal,* and Fishman was a financial columnist for the *New York Times.*

Barrett introduced the people with him and proceeded to describe the activities of the Sage ring and the murders that had taken place. He also talked about the involvement of TM and Cooper and how the ring had gotten TM placed on the country's highest terrorist list.

"We have in custody a man who is being charged with the murder of Mr. Morgan's daughter. He's at Evanston Hospital being treated for gunshot wounds he received when he tried to kill this man."

He pointed at TM.

"You are here because we don't know who we can trust in the federal government," he concluded.

All the while the reporters were tapping notes into their tablets. With their smartphones, they took several photographs of Morgan, TM, and Cooper and then asked several questions, particularly of Morgan. Finally they asked if they could use separate offices to contact their editorial desks.

59

Chief Inspector Diaz stepped up to the podium and announced the creation of a new fund to benefit the families of police officers killed or wounded in the line of duty. He said the fund was made possible by a donation of one million dollars. When asked who made the donation, he said the donor wished to remain anonymous.

TM and Cooper were sitting at a table in the dining area of the Evanston Hilton Garden Inn having breakfast. On the table before them were copies of that morning's *New York Times* and *Wall Street Journal*. The Sage story was highlighted on the front page of both newspapers and included photographs of Morgan, TM, and Cooper.

"I already had a call from my boss," Cooper said. "He saw the news last night and my name was mentioned. He said the governor had called him congratulating him on the role DPS played in exposing the Sage ring."

"He sure changed his tune from what he was saying to you last week."

"What are you going to do now?" Cooper asked.

"For the foreseeable future, I'll be dealing with the people who are trying to protect me until I've finished providing testimony.

Hopefully I can soon go back to Colorado and do my work. I could use a helper. Why don't you come to Colorado with me?"

"Just to work there?"

"I had something more in mind. Like maybe a partner in more ways than one."

Cooper looked at him and was silent.

"I'm torn," she finally said. "I'm very fond of you, but I'm not ready to give up my career. Can we visit each other from time to time?"

"Of course," TM said, knowing it was unlikely their visits would continue very long. He paused and then said, "We've been through so much. All because of a missing coed."

www.ingramcontent.com/pod-product-compliance
Lightning Source LLC
LaVergne TN
LVHW050613100826
845148LV00011B/1568

* 9 7 8 0 6 1 5 8 4 5 1 4 2 *